Flip Flops & Fast Laps

Pinned Wide Open

By: Tuesday Monroe

Dedication

For the girls in flip-flops who walk like they own the damn starting line.
Who love like fire, ride like chaos,
and make legends fall to their knees.

For the girls who don't flinch when the engines rev,
who don't soften just because someone calls them soft.
The ones who flirt like it's a game—
and win it like a war.

For the girls who kiss like they've got nothing to lose,
who text filthy at midnight and still get shit done by morning.
Who turn heartbreak into gasoline
and use it to torch the next mile.

This one's for the girls who didn't ask permission—
and wouldn't take it if it was offered.
Who don't just sit pretty in the passenger seat—
they grab the wheel, slam the throttle, and never look back.

To the wild ones.
To the fierce ones.
To the Flip-Flops who made the racer fall.

You are the spark.
You are the storm.
You are the whole damn track.

Flip Flops & Fast Laps: Pinned Wide Open
By Tuesday Monroe

© 2025 Copyright
All rights reserved. No part of this publication may be reproduced, stored in a retrieval system, or transmitted in any form or by any means—electronic, mechanical, photocopy, recording, or otherwise— without the prior written permission of the author, except for the use of brief quotations in a book review or scholarly journal.

First Edition: June 2025
ISBN: 9798289588708
Printed in the United States of America
K. Gerdes

Disclaimer:
This is a work of fiction. Names, characters, places, and incidents are either the product of the author's imagination or are used fictitiously. Any resemblance to actual persons, living or dead, events, or locales are entirely coincidental.

INTRODUCTION

This story doesn't start with fairy dust or glass slippers.

It starts with grit under your nails, calloused hands gripping handlebars, and a girl in flip-flops daring fate to flinch first.

It's not about perfection. It's about passion.
It's about crashing and climbing back on, bruised and breathless—
not because you have something to prove,
but because quitting was never in your damn blood.

This book is about love—the kind that's messy and maddening, full of late-night texts and race-day tension.
It's about the boy who rides like he's got demons to outrun.
And the girl who doesn't run at all.

It's about chaos and chemistry. Loyalty and lust. Slow kisses and fast engines.

So buckle up, baby.

Whether you came for the love story, the roar of the track, or the dirty talk between chapters—you're in the right place.

Because this isn't just another romance.

This is fire and fuel. This is *The Flip-Flops Edition*.

And you're about to see exactly what happens
when a man made of speed falls for a girl who makes the ground shake without ever lacing up her shoes.

Content

Chapter 1: Throttle Problems
Chapter 2: Bonfires & Bad Ideas
Chapter 3: Good Trouble
Chapter 4: Trouble in Aisle 5
Chapter 5: Karts & Chemistry
Chapter 6: Crash Course
Chapter 7: Red Flags & Race Flags
Chapter 8: Podium Promises & Dinner Dangers
Chapter 9: Heat Laps & Home Turf
Chapter 10: Throttle The Curve
Chapter 11: Pancake Promises & Pitfalls
Chapter 12: Dinner & Other Dangerous Things
Chapter 13: Too Perfect, Too Soon
Chapter 14: Reality Check, Party of One
Chapter 15: Headlines & Headaches
Chapter 16: The Away Game
Chapter 17: Race Night
Chapter 18: The Flashbulb
Chapter 19: Twist Me, Don't Test Me
Chapter 20: Cockblocked by Carbs
Chapter 21: Full Throttle & Front Row
Chapter 22: Cool Down Laps & Close Calls
Chapter 23: Promises & Pasta
Chapter 24: First Place. Fast Hands.
Chapter 25: Couchlight Confessions
Chapter 26: Dream Dirty. Stay Soft.
Chapter 27: Waffles & Whispers
Chapter 28: Win Me. Wreck Me.
Chapter 29: Raceday Residue
Chapter 30: Storm Warning
Chapter 31: Heat Check
Chapter 32: Tethered
Chapter 33: The Long Goodbye
Chapter 34: Signal Lost
Chapter 35: Final Lap

Chapter 1

Throttle Problems

The thing about backstage passes is no one tells you you'll also get full access to public humiliation. Margaret Mae Moley—Mae to the world, Maggie to her mother, and "Jesus, woman" to her ex—had managed to do the unthinkable: snag two VIP motocross passes for her ten-year-old son Beckett's birthday. Full pit access. Meet-the-riders. Front-row bleachers. The whole nine muddy, chaotic yards.

The problem? No one warned her that motocross riders travel in packs. Shirtless, tattooed, cocky-as-hell packs. "Mom, hurry up!" Beckett tugged her hand, already ten steps ahead with his lanyard swinging and a GoPro strapped to his chest like he was storming a beach in Normandy. "We're gonna miss the tire change demo!" "Becks, I swear to God, if you make me run in flip-flops again—" Too late, Her feet slapped against concrete like wet fish. She was chasing him through the paddock area, dodging scooters, camera crews, and enough sweaty testosterone to fog up a mirror at 100 yards. That's when it happened.

She turned a corner, mid-sprint, and slammed chest-first into a human wall. Not just a wall. A literal Greek-statue-sculpted, holy-triceps, vengeance-in-a-hoodie **man**. He caught her. Technically. One strong arm around her waist, the other steadying his own smoothie that was now dripping down both of them. "You okay there, flip-flops?" he asked, voice rough and amused. Mae looked up into eyes so dark and sharp they could've sliced her leggings right off. Which would've been fine, considering they were currently soaked in mango protein shake. "Define 'okay.' Because I just tackled a protein shake and it won." He smirked. Of course he did. With that jawline, he was probably born smirking. "Damn," he said, letting her go but not really moving. "You hit hard for someone who looks like a beach bonfire and trouble." Beckett popped up beside them, panting. "Holy crap, Mom! You just body-checked Trace Jagger!" Mae blinked. "I body-checked *who*?"

Trace Jagger. Six-time champion. The motocross king. Sponsor magnet. Every woman's fantasy—and every dad's nightmare. He was the reason Beckett had a poster on the ceiling. Because apparently motivation was best delivered in Monster Energy logos. Trace gave a casual wave to Beckett. "She caught me off guard. I'll forgive her if she gives me her towel." "I don't have a towel." "Then I'll take your number." Mae opened her mouth. Closed it. Blushed. Then immediately cursed herself for blushing. Beckett stepped in. "She doesn't give out her number to strangers. She says that's how you end up on a Dateline special." Trace laughed. Full-on, head-tilt-back, throat-exposed laugh. "Smart kid." "He's ten," Mae muttered. "He thinks cheese sticks are a balanced breakfast."

Trace leaned in slightly. "And what do *you* think?" "I think this entire encounter has derailed my afternoon, ruined my outfit, and possibly made me ovulate." Trace didn't miss a beat. "I aim to please." A handler called his name from across the paddock. Trace looked over, then back at her. "You gonna be around?" he asked, pulling off his hoodie and offering it to her. She took it—because holy hell it smelled like sweat, pine, and sins. "Maybe," she said. He winked. *Winked.* Like some sort of lust demon with a Red Bull contract. Then he jogged off, towel-snap flirting with a mechanic as he passed. Mae turned to Beckett. "Did I just get hit on by Trace-freaking-Jagger?" Beckett stared up at her like she'd just announced she was actually a transformer. "Can I put this on my Instagram?"

Later that night, after Beckett had fallen asleep mid-video edit, Mae curled up on the hotel bed in Trace's hoodie, legs tangled in too-warm sheets, fingers absentmindedly twirling the drawstring near her lips. Her hair was still damp from a shower, her face scrubbed clean, but her brain refused to quiet down. Every time she closed her eyes, she saw that cocky smirk. Heard his laugh. Felt the solid heat of his chest as he caught her like she weighed nothing. A girl could lose a lot of sleep fantasizing about a grip like that—and a voice like bourbon poured over gravel.

Why the hell hadn't she asked for his number? Or at least tackled him again with intention this time? Mae groaned and flipped her pillow, shoving her face into the cool side. The hoodie still smelled like him. Like pine, sweat, and temptation in fabric form. And against all logic, it made her ache in places she hadn't acknowledged in a long, long time. She told herself she'd forget about him. That, guys like Trace Jagger lived on magazine covers and podiums, not in the lives of single moms with flip-flop tans and overdue credit card bills. But fate, as it turns out, wasn't done with her.

The next morning, Mae walked into her neighborhood gym with sore legs, tragic leggings, and the kind of energy only four hours of sleep and a five-dollar gas station coffee could provide. She wasn't there to flirt. Or to think about cocky motocross legends who smelled like lust and danger. She was there to sweat out bad decisions and maybe, just maybe, pretend that the hoodie hanging off her back didn't still reek of sin. She made it through five minutes on the treadmill before someone stepped onto the machine beside hers. Large. Tall. Built like someone who didn't skip leg day—or any day.

Trace. Jagger. In the sweat-slicked, towel-slinging, protein-shaking, soul-wrecking flesh. Mae blinked like she was seeing a ghost. A really attractive, really smirky ghost. He looked over, all casual charm and sinful forearms, and said, "Well, well. If it isn't flip-flops." She tripped on air. Nearly flung herself off the treadmill like a ragdoll. "Are you stalking me now?" she gasped, slamming the emergency stop button. "Please," he said, tossing a towel over his shoulder and adjusting his incline like this was just any Monday. "You're the one who tackled me. I'm the victim."

"Victim of my sports bra's structural failure," she muttered, already regretting her outfit—and her life. "It was brave," he said with a slow grin. "I respect a woman who risks spontaneous bounce for speed." She laughed. Loudly. Too loudly. The old guy in the corner stretching his hamstring gave her a side-eye like she was disrupting yoga hour. But she couldn't help it. The man had a gift—for flirtation and chaos, wrapped in sweat and smugness. And dear god, he smelled good again. Not the pine and sin from yesterday. This was post-workout Trace. Muskier. Raw. Dangerous in a new way. Mae yanked her hoodie tighter around her waist, trying not to think about the fantasies she had last night involving shower steam, slippery tile, and that exact grin.

"I'm in town for two weeks," he said, casually adjusting the incline like he hadn't just made her core temperature spike. "Let me take you out." Mae raised an eyebrow. "Just like that? You body-check a woman, give her one hoodie, and suddenly she's your dinner date?" "Worked for the hoodie," he said, voice dipped in that easy cockiness that made her want to both kiss and strangle him. She snorted, slowing her treadmill pace and glancing sideways. "You're not even from here. What would be the point?" "Fun? Food? Mutual flirtation? Possibly a table-shaking good time?" Mae's laugh came out sharp, amused. "Wow, you really are confident." "I have skills." "And I have boundaries." He grinned wider, clearly not discouraged. "So that's a maybe?"

"That is very reluctant maybe. You get one date, Jagger. One. And only because you owe me a smoothie." Trace placed a hand over his heart like she'd just knighted him. "One smoothie. One date. One maybe. Got it." "And keep your table-shaking ego in check." "No promises." Trace's grin was slow and sinful. And just like that, Mae's dry spell screeched to a halt. She had two weeks. And something told her—Trace Jagger could fill every damn minute.

Chapter 2

Bonfires & Bad Ideas

"I don't need a date," Mae said out loud to her reflection. Her reflection, wearing Trace Jagger's hoodie and nothing else, looked back with the kind of smug that belonged in a romcom montage. Her hair was a wild halo, lips still pink from nervous lip-biting, and her eyes—well, they looked suspiciously like someone who was already halfway gone over a man she barely knew. She pulled the hoodie tighter for a second before yanking it off like it had personally offended her ovaries. Tossed it into the laundry basket as if that would erase the memory of how it had clung to her last night. The cotton was soft, oversized, warm—and traitorous. This was fine. Totally fine. It was just a date. With a motocross legend who smelled like sin and had a smirk that could get a nun to unbutton something. Casual. Except it didn't feel casual. It felt like every nerve ending in her body had RSVP'd to this date and brought a plus-one. Her stomach fluttered in ways it hadn't since high school. Her skin felt too tight. Her brain kept replaying every word he'd said at the gym—every look like it was branded. And it wasn't just attraction. That would've been easy. This was worse. This was *anticipation*.

She took a deep breath, slapped some tinted moisturizer on her face, and reminded herself she was a grown woman, not a hormonal teen. And yet, when she caught herself smiling for no reason—she knew she was screwed. She grabbed her phone.

Mae: I swear if this ends with me in jail or pregnant, I'm blaming you.

Tori: That was always the goal. Jail or babies. Maybe both.

Mae: That is not comforting.

Tori: Shut up and shave your legs. I packed Beckett's overnight bag. He's hyped for the sleepover. Go get yours, Flip-Flops.

Trace picked her up in a matte black Bronco that looked like it belonged to a Bond villain with a surfboard addiction. The headlights cut through the dusk like the opening scene of a music video—moody, dangerous, and undeniably hot. She opened the door and blinked at the interior, which smelled like leather, danger, and a dash of coconut air freshener. "Is this street legal?" "Probably not in several countries," he said, resting one tattooed arm on the wheel. "But it's sexy, right?" She climbed in, the seat hugging her like it had no business being that comfortable. "Like most bad ideas," she muttered, buckling in.

The ride was criminally smooth. Windows down, evening breeze tangling her hair, and Trace's playlist vibrating through the speakers. It was all moody guitar riffs, angsty vocals, and nostalgic lyrics from bands she used to make out to in high school parking lots. She gave him a sideways glance. "So what's the plan, Jagger? Are you going to wine and dine me?" He shot her a grin that could've been outlawed in some states. "Nope. Beach, blanket, bonfire, and burgers. And maybe, if you behave, a cooler full of spiked lemonade." She crossed her arms, fighting a smile. "That sounds dangerously close to charming." "I'll try to keep that in check," he said, tapping the wheel with one hand as they turned down a sandy access road. "Wouldn't want to ruin my reputation." She watched his profile in the fading light—strong jawline, sun-kissed skin, that maddening five-o'clock shadow. He didn't look like trouble. He looked like the reward for surviving it.

    The beach was a private stretch of sand tucked behind a rusted gate and a row of windswept palms that looked like they belonged on a postcard—if postcards included questionable legal access and a man who grinned like he had backup plans for every kind of trouble. Mae climbed out barefoot, the cool sand pressing between her toes as Trace unloaded a folded blanket, a mini grill, two lawn chairs, and—because of course he did—a Bluetooth speaker shaped like a gas can. He moved with that lazy confidence of someone who knew exactly how good he looked doing things with his hands. "Do you do this often?" Trace shook out the blanket and laid it flat in the center of their makeshift setup. "Nope. First time. Usually I'm either training, racing, or icing a body part I forgot existed." Mae dropped into one of the chairs, watching the orange glow of the horizon melt into the sea. "Sounds glamorous." He gave a low chuckle, opening the grill and tossing on two prepped patties like he'd done this exact move before. "You'd be surprised. Lots of airport chili dogs, bus station bathrooms, and forgetting what city I'm in." "Sounds like my last road trip with Beckett. Minus the trophies and adoring fans." "I'd trade the trophies for beach burgers and someone who doesn't scream when I beat them at Mario Kart."

    They ate with their toes buried in sand and mouths full of sarcasm. Every bite was paired with a quip. Every sip of lemonade sparked a comeback. And Mae, who normally carried armor made of wit and mom-responsibility, found herself leaning into the moment like it was her favorite kind of fiction. She kept waiting for it to turn awkward. For the silence to press in. But it didn't. It was just... easy. It was just... fun. And fun hadn't been on the menu for her in a long damn time. Not since the divorce. Not since the mental exhaustion of being both bad cop and good cop to a ten-year-old who thought life was best experienced on two wheels. Trace popped the cooler open and passed her a can, condensation sliding down the side. His hand lingered near hers a moment too long. "To spontaneous combustion." Mae tapped her can against his, watching the flames lick higher in the firepit beside them. "To bad decisions with good jawlines," she said, and took a sip. Trace's laugh rumbled low and pleased. "Hope you're ready, Flip-Flops. I specialize in both."

They watched the sun dip below the horizon, streaking the sky with molten gold and dusky wine. The last rays glinted off the ocean like it was hoarding secrets. The fire between them hissed and popped, casting flickering shadows across Trace's face—and damn it all, he looked even hotter in the firelight. Like a sin wrapped in salt and smoke. He sat back, one leg stretched out, forearm resting across a bent knee, drink balanced effortlessly in hand. The kind of man who looked like he was born for bonfires and bad decisions. Mae leaned on her elbow, watching him with open amusement, the flicker of heat under her skin matched only by the flames beside them. "You're staring, Flip-Flops," he said without looking over.

She didn't bother to look away. Her gaze trailed unapologetically down the line of his neck to where the white tee clung to him like it had been custom-stitched by a Greek god's thirsty assistant. "You wore a white t-shirt, brought tequila, and sat there like you invented the smolder. What exactly were you expecting?" He turned to face her then, a slow, knowing smirk tugging at his lips. "Or do you just like watching me sweat?" She took a long sip, held his gaze. "Both. Obviously. Now shut up." He shifted slightly, closing the space between them by an inch. Maybe two. The firelight licked the edges of his smirk. "Make me."

The tension thickened, taut as a wire pulled tight. Mae's mouth parted—somewhere between a retort and something reckless. Trace leaned in just enough for her to feel the heat radiating from his skin, his eyes zeroed in on her lips like he was calculating their exact distance. Her breath caught. "You're not allowed to kiss me yet." He didn't pull back. Just stayed there—hovering. Watching her like he could taste the next move. "Not even a little?" Her voice dipped. "Earn it." He sat back with a low laugh, dragging a hand through his hair. It should've felt like a victory, but instead, it felt like she'd poured gasoline on a flame just to admire how close she could get before it burned.

She cracked open another can, masking her fluster with bravado. "You're used to women throwing themselves at you, huh? Spoiler alert—I don't throw." Trace raised a brow, clearly amused. "You tackled me once already. You'll do it again." "Only if you deserve it." He tilted his head, eyes raking over her like a slow burn. "Challenge accepted." He grinned like a man already planning exactly how to earn it. And somewhere in the back of Mae's mind, a very rational voice whispered, *You're in trouble.*

Chapter 3

Good Trouble

Mae didn't remember falling asleep, but she remembered waking up. Not in a bed. Not in a mess of tangled sheets and sin, tangled in limbs and whispered promises. In a lawn chair. On the beach. Wrapped in Trace Jagger's hoodie—warm, oversized, and smelling like salt and his skin. It was slung around her like a promise no one had spoken aloud. Her neck was stiff. Her spine protested. But what struck her first wasn't the ache or the chill. It was the eerie quiet of the early morning, the kind that wrapped around you like a secret. The kind of silence that made you realize something had shifted overnight—something small, but irreversible.

The ocean murmured nearby, its waves lazy and soft. Above her, seagulls wheeled in the pale lavender sky, and she could taste the salt on her lips like a leftover dare. Her legs were draped over one armrest, her hair an absolute wreck, and her heart already doing too much despite the stillness. And yet... she didn't move. Didn't panic. Didn't scramble to check her phone or fix her face. For the first time in a long time, she simply existed—in the quiet, in the comfort, in someone else's scent clinging to her like it had a right to.

For a split second, before her eyes even opened fully, she felt warm. Safe. The kind of stillness that only came from being held—even if she hadn't been. Then came the stiff joints, the dry mouth, and the emotional whiplash that followed like a hangover. Her body ached in ways that had nothing to do with the chair and everything to do with what hadn't happened. The fire had burned low to embers. A sliver of early morning light hovered just over the water, cool and gray-blue. Her mouth was dry. Her back hurt. And her thighs—oh god, her thighs—were definitely not meant for sleeping in a half-upright position.

She looked over. Trace. Sprawled out on the blanket like he belonged to the morning. One arm slung lazily over his eyes, the other bent behind his head as if he'd drifted off mid-thought. His shirt was slightly wrinkled, the hem twisted up just enough to show a slice of golden skin and that ridiculous line of definition she'd been trying not to think about. His hair was an artful mess—like he'd just stepped out of bed and into a magazine spread—and his jawline wore scruff like it had been painted on by temptation itself. He looked peaceful. Too peaceful. Like the kind of man who didn't toss and turn with regrets. Like the kind of man who didn't know how loud he'd just echoed in someone else's head. Which was infuriating.

Because Mae? Mae looked like an abandoned mermaid who lost her dignity and her concealer in the same tide. She shifted in her chair, and the squeak of it made him stir. Trace blinked, squinted at her, then grinned. "You still here, Flip-Flops?" She rubbed her eyes. "Unfortunately." He propped himself up on an elbow, and Mae had to physically stop her gaze from dragging over the V of his shirt as it sagged open. She bit the inside of her cheek, willing herself not to ogle the abs that hinted through the fabric. She didn't need that kind of distraction. Not this early. Not when her resolve was already whisper-thin. "You cold? You stole my hoodie like a criminal." She lifted it slightly. "Well, you body heat-trapped me into a nap, so." He chuckled, voice low and warm. "Pretty sure you heat-trapped yourself." She ignored the ache between her legs and focused on the much safer ache in her neck. "How do you not look like roadkill after sleeping outside?" He shrugged. "Skill. Also—genetics." "You're obnoxious." "You like it." She hated that he was right.

By the time they made it back to her place, the sun was in full smug mode, glaring down like it knew exactly what hadn't happened but almost did. The kind of heat that made her skin too aware of itself, of where his hand had brushed hers during cleanup, of how close he'd stood when they folded the blanket. Trace helped unload her beach bag and the leftovers from their cookout. It should have felt awkward. It should've felt like the end of something temporary. But it didn't. It felt... familiar. Comfortable. Dangerous in the way a slippery slope is dangerous when you're already leaning too far forward.

She opened her front door and paused, her fingers resting on the knob a second longer than necessary. "You want coffee?" He leaned against the doorframe, one arm braced above him, the other slung casually in his pocket like the answer was already yes. "You offering because you want to, or because you feel bad you didn't let me kiss you?" She stepped inside, the air-conditioned calm of her home brushing over her sun-warmed skin. "Both," she said, tossing her keys into the bowl with practiced indifference that didn't quite match the chaos in her chest. He followed, steps slow, easy. Like he knew exactly how to fill a space without overtaking it. Like this wasn't his first time walking into someone else's guarded world.

She moved through the kitchen with a strange, deliberate rhythm—like if she kept her hands busy, her thoughts wouldn't betray her. She brewed the coffee while he leaned on the counter, his gaze fixed not just on her face but on her movements. The tilt of her head. The way her bottom lip caught between her teeth when she measured the grounds. Every once in a while, he'd reach over and adjust something—push her phone out of the coffee splash zone, tug a tea towel back into place, swipe a crumb off the edge of the counter. Like he'd done it a thousand times. Like he'd lived there once and still knew where everything belonged. Mae poured two mugs and handed him one, her fingers grazing his just long enough to set her pulse thudding in her ears. She wasn't even sure if he meant to touch her like that—gentle, deliberate, distracting.

But her body betrayed her—heartbeat skipping, breath catching, stomach twisting in on itself. She told herself it was just contact. Just skin. A meaningless brush between two people who knew better than to let it mean something. But her chest was tight with something unnamed, sharp and tender. And all she could think was: *Don't fall. Not yet.* He sipped. "Damn. You make strong coffee." "Single mom. I take my caffeine the way I take my men—hot and with absolutely no patience." He laughed. And she swore it vibrated straight down her spine.

Trace didn't stay long. Just long enough to lean against her kitchen counter like he'd done it before. To smirk at the way her hair was barely holding together with a chewed-up hair tie. To say something like, "Messy buns and that smart mouth? Dangerous combo, Moley," while sipping his coffee like it was just another Tuesday. He teased her about stealing his hoodie. She fired back about him drooling in his sleep. They danced around the tension like it wasn't sitting between them with its arms crossed, waiting.

Then, just when she thought maybe he'd say something serious—something she wasn't ready to hear—he set his mug in her sink, winked, and said, "See you around, Flip-Flops." And he left. Not rushed. Not lingering. Just... gone. Like it was no big deal. Which, for her, was a very big deal. And Mae stood in her kitchen, barefoot, holding an empty coffee mug and wondering what the hell just happened. It wasn't a date. It wasn't a hookup. It wasn't anything, really. Except that it felt like something. Something potent. Charged. Like someone had lit a match inside her chest and walked away whistling. Like her heart had taken a step she hadn't agreed to, but her body had followed anyway. Like a door had opened in her chest that she hadn't realized was locked. A door she'd boarded up after the last time she let someone see too far inside. And now it was wide open—no warning, no permission—letting in all the light and heat and possibility she'd trained herself to ignore. Like her body recognized a rhythm her brain didn't want to acknowledge. One she hadn't danced to in years. One that made her feel alive in a way she hadn't dared want for a long, long time. Something that might be trouble. The kind that doesn't knock—just barges in, barefoot and grinning. Good trouble. And damn it, she wanted more. Which meant she was screwed.

Chapter 4

Trouble in Aisle 5

Trace wasn't supposed to haunt her grocery run. And yet, there he was—on a promo poster for an upcoming motocross meet, grinning like the smug devil that he was, arms crossed over his chest like he hadn't just lit her nerves on fire and walked out like it was no big deal. Mae glared at the sign, then sighed and pushed her cart harder down the aisle like she could physically escape him. She needed eggs. Oat milk. Not a full-blown identity crisis. She rounded the corner into produce and nearly rammed her cart into a pyramid of avocados. A voice behind her drawled, "You always shop angry, or is that just a Tuesday thing?" Mae froze. Swiveled. And there he was. Trace Jagger.

Wearing a hoodie, sunglasses on top of his head, and holding a container of strawberries like it owed him money. His hair was slightly messy, like he'd run a hand through it a dozen times that morning. His grin was instant—and criminal. "Are you stalking me?" she asked, already backing up an inch. "In my defense, I saw the fruit tower first. You just happened to be rage-pushing your way into it." "I am not rage-pushing." "You're definitely rage-pushing. You almost murdered a banana display." She rolled her eyes, but her mouth twitched. "You don't live here. What are you still doing in my grocery store?" "Two-week training. And I needed coffee. Then I needed groceries. Then I needed to make sure Flip-Flops hadn't fallen off the face of the earth." "Well, congratulations. Flip-Flops is alive and aggressively price-matching oat milk." He smiled. That same low-grade heart attack of a smile. "Dinner," he said. She blinked. "Excuse me?" "Tonight. You. Me. Real food. Not beach burgers or gas station coffee." Mae hesitated. She could hear Tori in her head already: *Say yes. Then tell me every damn detail.* "I have Beckett tonight." "So bring him. My treat. I'm great with kids." "He's not a rescue dog." "I wasn't suggesting he sit at my feet." She narrowed her eyes. "Fine. But we're picking the place. Somewhere public. And no tequila." "You say that like tequila's the villain." "You're the villain. Tequila's your henchman." He grinned wider. "Then I guess I'll see you at six." Mae watched him saunter off, strawberries in hand, and hated—truly hated—how much she liked the way he walked away.

Back home, Beckett was mid-video game and halfway through a bag of pretzels, controller in hand and mouth full of crunch, when Mae hovered in the doorway and cleared her throat with practiced mom-level intensity. "You remember Trace Jagger?" Beckett didn't even look away from the screen. "Duh. He's basically a motocross god. Why? Did he sign my helmet or something? Did you see him again? Did he say something about me?" Mae leaned against the doorframe, arms crossed, trying to look casual and failing. "He invited us to dinner." That got his attention. The controller hit pause mid-jump, and Beckett slowly turned to face her like she'd just told him Santa Claus and Tony Hawk were co-hosting a sleepover. "Wait. You're saying I get to eat dinner with *Trace Jagger*? In public? Like a real restaurant? Where, other people can see me?" "Yes. If you wear a clean shirt, use deodorant, and don't ask him anything about his tattoos until after dessert." Beckett fist-pumped like he'd just won the championship. "This is the best day of my life. Can I bring my GoPro? Do you think he'll race me in the parking lot? Should I ask him if he wants to help me fix my suspension?" "No. No. And absolutely not. Eat your pretzels."

Mae walked away before he could ask if he should bring a Sharpie. She passed the hallway mirror on her way to the bathroom and paused, staring at her reflection like she was trying to recognize the woman blinking back. Her hair was a windblown mess from the day, her t-shirt slightly stretched at the neckline, and a smear of pretzel salt clung to the corner of her mouth. Was she really doing this again? Letting a man—*that man*—into her world, even temporarily? Letting herself feel a flicker of possibility when she'd spent years carefully extinguishing every spark before it could catch flame? She exhaled slowly, like the breath might settle the nerves humming just beneath her skin.

In the bathroom, she opened the drawer where her barely-used makeup stash lived like it was an artifact from a former life. A dusty compact, half-dried mascara, a bronzer palette she'd bought on clearance last spring. She dabbed a little color into her cheeks, curled her lashes. Swiped on balm with more precision than she cared to admit. She wasn't going full glam. That wasn't her anymore. But she also wasn't going in looking like motherhood had chewed her up and spit her out in leggings and exhaustion. Just mascara. Maybe a little bronzer. Definitely deodorant. A spritz of body spray she hadn't worn since her last girls' night with Tori. And maybe—*maybe*—shaved her legs. Not because she expected anything. But because it made her feel ready. Aware. Awake. Just in case. Because something told her this wasn't going to be just dinner. It was going to be a memory. The kind you replay later when the house is quiet. The kind that lingers. The kind that sticks in your memory. Or worse—your heart.

Chapter 5

Karts & Chemistry

Mae should've known Trace wouldn't pick a normal restaurant. Six o'clock, sharp. She pulled into the parking lot of *The Pit Stop Diner*—a chrome-and-neon joint attached to an indoor kart track whose slogan read, **"Refuel & Race."** The glow of the sign bounced off polished motorcycles lined up like trophies outside, and engines revved every few seconds as riders hit quick laps before grabbing burgers. Beckett practically vibrated out of the passenger seat. "They have electric karts inside, Mom! Look—there's a leaderboard!" Mae exhaled, smoothed her sundress, and reminded herself she'd survived childbirth—she could survive dinner with a motocross legend in a glorified speedway cafeteria. Trace was waiting just outside the glass doors. He wore dark jeans, a charcoal henley that did dangerous things to her pulse, and a grin that said *I knew you'd show.* He squatted to Beckett's level first—a move that punched admiration straight through Mae's chest. "Hey, champ. Ready to crush a double bacon?" Beckett's jaw unhinged. "You know my order?" Trace tapped his temple. "I pay attention." Then he looked up at Mae and, in a softer voice only she could hear, added, "Always." Her knees went warm. Great. Off to a stellar start.

The hostess—a pierced college kid with bubble-gum hair—lit up when she recognized Trace. "Holy crap! You're on the poster in the lobby. Table for three?" "Four," Trace corrected. "My mechanic's swinging by later to grab a milkshake—he'll sit at the bar." Mae raised an eyebrow. *Smooth. Extra seat beside me, is that the play?* They were escorted to a booth shaped like a half-keg. Neon track-maps adorned the walls; every few minutes, a bell rang overhead announcing lap records. Beckett slid in first, eyes on the digital scoreboard rotating above the order window. Mae followed, leaving Trace the outer seat—easy escape if he felt claustrophobic under the weight of her second-guessing. A waitress named *Shelby* appeared, wielding an iPad. She did a double take at Trace, then glanced at Mae as if confirming the legend was, indeed, on a date with a mortal. "Drinks?" "Root beer float," Beckett blurted. Mae ordered water, and Trace asked for "whatever craft IPA pairs with maternal skepticism." Shelby laughed too loudly and almost knocked over the ketchup.

While Beckett debated between a pretzel-bun burger and chicken-n-waffle sliders, Trace rested an elbow on the back of the booth, turning his body toward Mae. Close, but not touching. "You look... different out of flip-flops," he murmured. She smoothed the hem of her dress. "They were in the wash. Sue me." "I was going to say you look beautiful." Heat bloomed in her cheeks. She hid it by stealing Beckett's menu and pretending to examine milkshake flavors. Beckett finally chose the bacon monstrosity. Mae picked the grilled salmon bowl, determined to cling to some semblance of adult nutrition. Trace ordered the blackened steak tacos and, when Shelby left, flicked his gaze to Mae's bare knees. "You shaved." Her fork clattered against the table. "Excuse you?" He leaned closer, lowering his voice so Beckett—now glued to the karts racing on wall-mounted TVs—couldn't hear. "Last night you had a tiny band-aid on your shin. It's gone. Either you healed miraculously... or you shaved." She swallowed. Hard. "Observant, aren't you?" "About you? Yeah." She would've fired back, but Beckett interrupted: "Trace, what's your favorite tattoo?" Trace straightened. "Probably the compass on my shoulder." He tugged the collar of his henley aside, revealing inked cardinal points wrapped around coordinates. "It's the track where I won my first Supercross title." Beckett gawked. "That is sick!" He turned to Mae. "Can I get a compass tattoo?" Mae deadpanned, "Sure. On your eighteenth birthday. *2033*." Trace laughed. A real, belly-deep sound that made Mae's pulse jitter.

Their meals arrived alongside a modest parade of curious diners asking for selfies. To Mae's surprise, Trace obliged every single one—standing for photos, signing napkins, even drawing a tiny dirt bike on a toddler's cast. When the last fan left, Mae said, "You're good with them." He shrugged. "They keep the lights on. Plus, I like people." She arched her brow. "Even sarcastic single moms?" "Especially sarcastic single moms." Beckett inhaled his burger, then bounced in the seat. "Trace, can we hit the kart track *pleeease?*" He pointed to a sign: **Family Heats – $15 per kart.'** Mae opened her mouth to veto—bedtime, budgets—but Trace slipped a card onto the table. "Three karts, fifteen laps. Loser buys dessert." Beckett squealed. "Mom, you're going down." Mae narrowed her eyes. "I drive a minivan, kid. That's basically a land yacht. You sure you want this smoke?" Trace's grin turned wicked. "Oh, I want all the smoke."

Ten minutes later, Mae sat in a blue electric kart, helmet hair already imminent. Beckett occupied the red kart beside her, bouncing despite the seat belt. Trace slid into the black kart at the front, looking entirely too confident. The lights above the starting line shifted from red to yellow to green. Beckett shot forward with a shriek. Mae punched the pedal and fishtailed, tires squealing. Trace held back, matching her speed, letting Beckett take the early lead. Mae glanced over at him on a hairpin, eyes narrowing. "You're sandbagging." He winked through his visor. "Ladies first." Competitive fire roared to life. She gunned the throttle, passing Beckett on the straightaway. Her son whooped and tailed her draft. Lap six, Trace finally unleashed himself—darting ahead with professional precision, taking corners so tight his bumper kissed the guardrail. Lap ten, Mae clipped his rear tire, stealing second place; Beckett giggled maniacally behind them. Final lap, Trace shot past both of them on the last bend, crossing the line half a second ahead. Beckett rolled in, then Mae, laughing so hard she nearly missed the brake pedal. They exited their karts breathless, sweating, and high on adrenaline. Beckett leapt into Trace's arms. "That was epic!" Trace mussed the kid's hair. "You almost had me, champ." Mae planted hands on hips, panting. "I demand a rematch. Best two out of three." Trace's eyes glittered. "Any time, Flip-Flops."

True to the wager, Mae ordered dessert: two Oreo shakes and a salted-caramel for herself. They reclaimed their booth, cheeks still flushed. Beckett slurped noisily then blurted, "Are you two dating?" Mae choked on caramel foam. Trace wiped a lip of whipped cream, buying time. "We're... hanging out." He turned to Mae, expression gentle. "But I'd like to take your mom out again—maybe without an audience." Beckett's eyes sparkled. "Can I come?" Mae laughed, heart twisting. "Buddy, that defeats the purpose." Trace leaned closer, voice low. "I'm serious. Just you, next time." She held his gaze. "We'll see." But the smile tugging at her mouth made it sound like yes. Shelby delivered the bill. Trace grabbed it; Mae protested; Trace slid it higher out of reach. "Loser buys dessert. Rules are rules." "You're insufferable," she muttered. "Yet here you are."

They stepped into the night air, moonlight glinting off parked bikes. Beckett walked ahead, brandishing an invisible checkered flag while making engine noises. Trace stopped beside Mae's car, hands in pockets. "I had fun tonight." She nodded. "Me too." Nerves fluttered; she scanned the lot—no paparazzi, no fans—just the growl of engines from the track. Trace's gaze dipped to her lips. "Still a no on the kiss?" Mae's pulse jumped. "Earn it." He smiled, stepped back, and pressed something into her palm—a folded receipt. He closed her fingers over it, the touch brief but electric. "Next race," he said. "Tickets. Paddock passes. For you and Beckett. Come root for the villain."

Then, with an infuriating wink, he jogged toward a motorcycle, revved the engine, and shot into the night—leaving Mae standing under the neon, heart drumming like a starting gate. She opened the receipt. *Two VIP passes. Sunday. 1 p.m.* On the back he'd written, **"Round two. –T"** Mae leaned against her van, grinning so wide her cheeks hurt. Yep. Definitely not *just* dinner. And definitely the kind of memory that lodges in your chest—and waits.

Chapter 6

Crash Course

The next morning, Mae woke to the sound of Beckett banging around in the kitchen, narrating his cereal-making like it was a YouTube cooking channel. "Step one," he called out. "Pour cereal before milk. Always. Rookie mistake if you don't." Mae groaned into her pillow. Her entire body felt sore—not from anything particularly sinful, but from go-kart whiplash and laughing too hard at Trace's jokes. Her cheeks still ached from smiling, and there was a very real possibility her heart had sprouted a crush that had nothing to do with high school posters or celebrity fantasy. It was *real.* And it was dangerous.

She rolled out of bed, tied her robe tighter than necessary, and shuffled into the kitchen. Beckett looked up with a spoon hanging out of his mouth. "Mom, can we go to every race from now on? Like, can we live on the motocross tour?" She grabbed a mug from the cabinet. "Sure. Right after we win the lottery and homeschool you in pit stops and tire changes." He grinned, completely undeterred. "You'd make a hot race mom. Like, in those black tank tops and boots." Mae nearly dropped her mug. "Beckett Alexander Moley, do not ever say the words 'hot race mom' again." He shrugged, still chewing. "Just sayin'."

She poured her coffee, trying to ignore the way her stomach flipped at the memory of Trace's voice. The way he'd leaned into her at the diner. The way he said her name, like it tasted better than dessert. Mae brewed her coffee and leaned against the counter, watching her son rattle off more stats about Trace's last race. He'd memorized the man's bike number, sponsors, and apparently his favorite breakfast sandwich. And it made something in her tighten. This wasn't just a crush for Beckett. It was a bond forming in real time. And if Trace disappeared? If he ghosted? That heartbreak wouldn't just be hers. She pulled out her phone, stared at it. No messages. Not that she expected one this early. Still… She texted Tori.

Mae: He invited us to his next race. VIP passes. Sunday.

Tori: And let me guess… he also handed you your ovaries on a receipt.

Mae: Something like that.

Tori: You shaving again?

Mae: Shut up.

Tori: Babe. If you're shaving before 10am, it's love. Or at least *lust with consistency.*

Mae laughed into her coffee. But underneath the sarcasm was that pit in her stomach. That whisper: *What if this is temporary? What if he doesn't stay?* Because the last time she let someone in this close, they'd walked away—and left her holding all the pieces. And this time, there was Beckett in the mix. She couldn't afford to gamble with her kid's heart.

After breakfast, Mae drove Beckett to school. He talked the whole ride about the track, about Trace's tattoos, and about wanting to grow his hair out to match him. She pulled up to the drop-off loop, kissed him goodbye, and sat for a moment in the quiet after he disappeared through the school doors. Her phone buzzed. **Unknown number.** Her heart kicked.

Trace: Hope you're free Sunday. Don't forget sunblock. And maybe something in team colors. We're red. ;)

A second later, a photo popped up. Trace, still in bed, hair wild, shirtless under the covers, holding up a coffee mug that said *BAD DECISIONS CLUB.* Mae choked on nothing, coughed into her steering wheel, and laughed until her ribs hurt.

She texted back: **You're a menace.**

Trace replied: **Takes one to know one. Bring Flip-Flops. He's my good luck charm.**

Mae leaned her head back against the headrest. Damn it. She was falling. And she didn't know how to stop.

That afternoon, she met Tori for iced coffees on the patio of their favorite cafe. Tori wore big sunglasses and a knowing smirk. "Tell me everything." Mae slumped into her chair. "It was supposed to be just dinner." Tori blew across her straw. "Babe, nothing about you and Trace Jagger is ever going to be just anything." "I know," Mae said, quieter than she meant. Tori studied her. "You like him." "I do." "You're scared." Mae nodded. "Because of Beckett?" "Because of everything. Because I've done this before. Because last time I believed someone's promises, I ended up alone with a toddler and court dates." Tori reached across the table, squeezed her hand. "You're not the same woman anymore. And Trace isn't that guy." "You don't even know him." "No," Tori agreed. "But I know you. And I know the look on your face when you say his name." Mae bit her lip, staring down into her cup. The ice had started to melt. "I want to believe it," she said. "But what if he walks away?" "Then he's a fool." Tori leaned in. "But what if he doesn't?"

That night, Mae couldn't sleep. She lay awake, staring at the ceiling fan, replaying everything. The way Trace looked at her. The way he talked to Beckett like he wasn't just tolerating a kid but *enjoying* him. The way her stomach flipped when he leaned in too close. This wasn't a fling. It couldn't be. Not when it already felt like the first thing in years that made her feel alive. And that's what scared her most. Because if she let herself fall, and he didn't catch her? It wouldn't be a stumble. It'd be a faceplant. And for once, Mae didn't know if she was brave enough to risk it. But then she thought about the VIP passes tucked in her purse. The look on Beckett's face when Trace talked to him like a future champion. The way her name sounded in his mouth. And maybe—*maybe*—for the first time in a long damn time, she wasn't just afraid of falling. She was afraid of never flying again.

Chapter 7

Red Flags & Race Flags

 Mae didn't usually wake up feeling like her life was a coming-of-age movie—but that morning? That morning, she stretched beneath fresh sheets, sunlight slipping through her blinds, and felt like something was about to shift. Race day. She sat up, blinked the sleep from her eyes, and was immediately tackled by the weight of two thoughts, first, her son was about to meet hundreds of dirt bike fans who worshipped Trace Jagger like a deity on two wheels. Second, she had no idea what to wear. "Beckett!" she shouted, already fumbling for coffee. "Do we even own anything red?" He raced into the kitchen, socks sliding on the floor, arms up like a tiny gladiator. "I made signs!" He held up two pieces of neon poster board covered in duct tape, glitter, and what appeared to be aggressively enthusiastic slogans like *#TeamTrace* and *Throttle the World!* Mae sipped coffee and blinked. "You've been up since what, 6?" "Five-thirty. I had to glue the lightning bolts." "Obviously."

 Mae ended up in her one red tank top, paired with jeans and a denim jacket she immediately regretted when she stepped outside and hit a wall of heat. Her nerves felt like they were tap dancing behind her ribs, each heartbeat louder than the last. Beckett, on the other hand, was in full fan mode—Trace's number painted on his cheek, his posters packed in the back seat, and a foam finger that was already shedding pieces of red fuzz on the floorboards. "Do you think Trace will let me hold his helmet?" he asked as she drove. "I think if you ask nicely and don't tackle him like last time, maybe." "I didn't tackle. I launched with enthusiasm." Mae smiled. "Noted."

By 11:45 a.m., they were pulling into the lot of the Redwood Raceway, a massive complex tucked between towering pine trees and dust clouds thick enough to taste. The scent of gasoline and sunscreen clung to the air like a second skin. The steady roar of engines built a soundtrack of chaos that vibrated straight through the steering wheel. It was like a small city had popped up overnight—pop-up tents flapping in the wind, grills sizzling with bratwursts, and foldout chairs arranged like tribal circles around mini coolers. There were people in team jerseys, kids racing around on scooters, and teenagers posing in front of branded trailers like they were in a motocross-themed fashion shoot.

Mae parked beside a camper with a decal of a flaming skull doing a wheelie and tried not to feel underdressed. Next to everyone in mesh-back hats and gearhead tanks, she felt like she'd shown up at a costume party dressed as "confused single mom in Target chic." Beckett, unfazed, wore the foam finger like it was a badge of honor. The glitter on his homemade posters sparkled under the noon sun. "VIP check-in," a security guy said, scanning the pass hanging from her neck. "You'll want to follow that row of tents. Pit access wristbands are over there." "Got it," Mae said, adjusting the strap on her crossbody bag and taking Beckett's hand.

They passed rows of shiny dirt bikes standing like soldiers, tires stacked in pyramids, and gear laid out like offerings to the gods of speed. Every few steps, someone shouted something unintelligible over the noise of revving engines. Beckett was practically vibrating. "Look at that helmet! Mom, that guy's wearing actual gold goggles! Did you see the stickers on that truck?!" He pointed at everything—bikes, trailers, tents with merch, even one booth selling tire-scented candles. "This is heaven," he whispered. Mae couldn't help but smile. It kind of was.

They found the VIP tent just as Trace emerged from behind one of the trailers, already in gear—black and red riding suit that hugged his frame in all the sinful ways, helmet hooked under one arm, hair slightly damp from warmups and wind. He looked like a walking adrenaline ad. Or the cover of a bad-boy romance novel someone would hide in a beach tote. Beckett dropped the poster like it was radioactive. Trace spotted them instantly. His face lit up like he hadn't just finished doing seventy mph over a berm. He jogged over with that signature swagger, the one that suggested he didn't just walk—he claimed space. "Flip-Flops! Kid Jagger!" he called out, grin wide and wild. "You made it. And with signs. Hell yeah. That's championship energy right there." Beckett immediately launched into a fist bump like they'd been teammates for years. "You're gonna destroy them today, right? Like, embarrass them?" Trace crouched down beside him, helmet balanced on one knee. "Every single one. I'll even make it look cool. Are you going to cheer loudly?" "I made throat-coating tea this morning so I don't lose my voice," Beckett said seriously, as if he were about to give a TED Talk on fan dedication.

Trace let out a whistle and looked up at Mae. "Obsessed. I love it. He's more prepared than my pit crew." She smirked, unable to stop the way her arms crossed—mostly to keep her hands from doing something like touching him. "He's been on a sugar high since 6 a.m. I'm terrified." Trace stood, close enough that she could see the edge of a bruise on his collarbone and the dimple threatening to break through his grin. "You look good in red." Mae raised an eyebrow. "You too." Trace laughed under his breath, head tilted like he was filing the moment away for later. Like he already had plans to make her say that again—but maybe with less distance between them.

The race started in twenty minutes. Trace led them to the paddock where a crew member gave Beckett a headset to listen to race audio. Trace ducked behind a screen to finish gearing up. Before disappearing, he turned to Mae. "After the race, there's a podium thing. Stick around. Then maybe... you, me, less dirt, real food?" "We'll see how you do out there, champ." His grin widened. "Brutal. I like it." The race was electric.

The engines snarled to life like beasts uncaged, a visceral wall of sound that slammed into Mae's chest and reverberated down to her bones. She and Beckett stood just behind the pit fencing, their view partially obscured by banners and bodies, but it didn't matter. The vibration in the air, the anticipation in the crowd—it was all a living, breathing thing. Trace shot out of the gate like a cannonball, his bike carving through the early chaos with ruthless precision. He immediately took the lead, all fluid angles and raw speed, a blur of red and black slicing the track. Beckett, through the headset clamped over his ears, was completely unhinged. "He took the inside corner! He's blocking number 32! MOM, HE'S A LITERAL NINJA." Mae was yelling too—half in shock, half in laughter—eyes flicking from turn to jump, heart suspended in her throat every time Trace leaned in hard or launched off a ramp like gravity was just a suggestion. She clutched the fencing like it could anchor her, adrenaline sparking in her bloodstream like she was out there too.

The pack behind him snarled and jostled, trying to close the gap, but Trace moved like he owned the dirt. Every turn was calculated. Every jump landed clean. He wasn't just fast—he was fierce, a storm on two wheels. "Look at that pass! LOOK AT IT!" Beckett's commentary was half-scream, half-miracle. By the final lap, the air had reached a fever pitch. Spectators screamed, leaned over rails, waved flags and signs. Mae could barely think, let alone speak. All she could do was feel—heart in freefall, lungs refusing full breaths, hands shaking around the foam coffee cup she'd long since forgotten was empty. Trace hit the final straight and flew across the finish line with a front-wheel pop and a trail of dust like a curtain call. The crowd erupted. Beckett threw both fists in the air and jumped so high he knocked over a cooler full of sparkling water. "HE DID IT! MOM! HE FREAKING DID IT!" Mae stood frozen, mouth open, chest aching with something she couldn't name. Pride, yes. Awe, absolutely. But there was something else beneath it—something that felt suspiciously like being seen. Like the man she'd barely let in had just made space for her in his spotlight. Trace had done it. And somehow, it felt like they had too.

Post-race, Trace was lifted onto the podium like a war hero—cheers rising like a wave, champagne spraying from every direction. Crew members hugged, cameras snapped, and the announcer's voice boomed across the stadium, praising every sharp turn and risky pass like it was a strategic masterpiece. Trace raised the trophy with one hand, helmet tucked under his other arm, and smiled with something that wasn't quite arrogance but definitely wasn't humility either. It was confidence—earned and blazing. Mae watched from below, shoulder to shoulder with other VIP spectators, but it felt like there was no one else around when Trace's eyes found hers. They locked across the chaos, heat and wildness still swirling around them. He didn't wave, didn't shout—just gave her a slow, unmistakable wink. Like he'd known she'd be there. Like it had all been for her. Mae felt her knees buckle slightly, the air thinning in her lungs.

Beckett looked up at her with wide, sparkly eyes. "Mom?" "Yeah?" "I think I want to be him when I grow up." Mae's gaze stayed locked on Trace, who hadn't looked away, who stared like she was the thing worth winning—not the race, not the trophy, but her. She swallowed, a smile catching at the corners of her lips. "Me too, buddy," she whispered. "Me too."

Chapter 8

Podium Promises & Dinner Dangers

Mae didn't realize she was still grinning until they were halfway to the parking lot and Beckett asked why she looked like she'd won a trophy too. Maybe she had. Maybe it wasn't gold or engraved, but something quieter. Something thudding behind her ribs. Trace Jagger was waiting by her car. He'd changed—well, mostly. His gear was gone, replaced by black joggers and a clean T-shirt stretched over his chest like it was made for it. Hair damp. Skin still flushed from the race. He looked like trouble on vacation. The casual kind that made you want to lean in and ruin your plans. Beckett launched toward him like a rocket. "THAT WAS INSANE. You were airborne for, like, half the track." Trace laughed, crouched, and let Beckett jabber through every second of his own personal sports recap. He listened, nodding like every syllable mattered.

Mae leaned against the car and crossed her arms. She watched the way Trace gave Beckett his full attention, the way his grin spread wide and genuine, and felt that pesky warmth in her chest expand like an overconfident balloon. When Beckett finally paused for air, Trace looked up at Mae. "Dinner still on the table?" "If you don't mind the company of someone who spilled sparkling water on three VIPs." He grinned. "That just means you'll keep things interesting."

Dinner was a beachside dive bar with picnic tables in the sand and string lights that blinked like fireflies. The menu was handwritten on a chalkboard. The vibe was barefoot and unbothered. Mae tried not to overthink how natural it felt to be there with them—how easy it was to fall into conversation, how she didn't feel the need to fill every silence, how Trace's eyes kept finding hers across the table. Trace ordered burgers, fries, and enough soda for Beckett to bounce off the dunes. The kid didn't stop grinning, even with a mouth full of waffle fry. "Have you ever crashed badly?" Beckett asked around a sip of root beer. "Couple times," Trace said. "Worst was a broken collarbone and four cracked ribs. And once I got a tire print across my back. Looked like a tattoo." "Cool," Beckett said reverently. "Did you cry?" "Like a baby," Trace admitted with a wink. Mae snorted into her drink. "At least you're honest."

Trace looked at her over the rim of his glass. "Always. Even when it's inconvenient." That look held too long. Long enough that Mae felt it like a low current beneath her skin. It buzzed through her ribs and settled somewhere south. "Trace said he used to train in Arizona," Beckett told her like it was classified intel. "In the desert. I Googled it once. The dirt there looks like Mars." "Hotter, too," Trace said, tearing into his burger. "Like cooking your kneecaps from the inside out." The three of them laughed, the kind of laugh that knocked walls down and let something new in. "Do you ever get scared?" Beckett asked. "Of crashing?" "Of, like... being bad at it one day." Trace's smile faltered for just a second, and Mae saw it—the vulnerability that flickered beneath the charm. Then it was gone, replaced by something softer. "Sure," Trace said. "But that's why I ride harder. If fear shows up, I let it ride shotgun. Just means I care enough to keep pushing." Beckett nodded like he'd just heard the meaning of life. Mae's heart clenched.

After dinner, they walked along the beach, Trace kicking off his shoes, Beckett trailing a stick through the sand like he was mapping a treasure hunt. The moon was rising. Soft. Golden. Mae couldn't remember the last time she'd seen the ocean at night without thinking about bills or bedtimes. They talked about nothing. Favorite cereals. Worst movie endings. The dumbest thing they'd ever done on a dare. (Mae's was trying to do the worm at a PTA meeting.) Beckett eventually dragged his sandy self back to the Bronco, too full and too happy to keep his eyes open. He curled up in the back seat with a foam finger over his face like a sleep mask. Trace leaned on the hood beside her. "He's cool. Like his mom." Mae arched a brow. "You don't even know me." "I know enough to want to." The tension stretched. Not heavy. Not awkward. Just full—like a storm waiting for permission to break. Mae looked down at the sand. "This isn't a forever thing." Trace shrugged. "Most good things aren't. Doesn't mean they're not worth it." She looked up. His eyes were on hers. Steady. Sure. Her brain screamed to be careful, to keep this temporary. But her body... her body just wanted more. And damn it, she wanted to know what it felt like to stop pretending she didn't care. So she kissed him. It was quick. Maybe too quick. A flash of salt and heat and impulse. But he chased it. Pulled her back in. Slower this time. Deeper. A kiss that tasted like the last lap of a race you didn't want to end. His hand found her waist. Hers gripped his shirt like she could anchor herself to the moment. When they finally pulled apart, Trace whispered against her lips, "Still not a forever thing. Just a really, really good night." Mae smiled. "We'll see."

They drove back with the windows down, the radio playing softly. Beckett snored in the backseat, Trace's hand rested on the console—close, but not quite touching hers. He walked them to the door. "You gonna ghost me again?" she asked as she unlocked it. "I don't ghost," he said. "I haunt." Mae laughed. "That's worse." He leaned in, brushing a kiss to her cheek. "You'll see me soon. I promise." She stepped inside and watched him walk back to the Bronco, muscles moving under soft cotton, like temptation on legs. Mae closed the door. Leaned against it. And smiled like an idiot into the dark.

Chapter 9

Heat Laps & Home Turf

Mae's alarm went off at 6:02 a.m., but she was already awake—staring at the ceiling, replaying last night's kiss like it was on an endless highlight reel. Her lips still tingled. Her pulse still rabbit-kicked. And somewhere in the living room, Beckett was humming the ESPN theme while packing lunch because he'd insisted on being "race-fuel responsible" now. Coffee. She needed coffee—and maybe a moment to breathe before real life chased the fantasy out the door. She shuffled into the kitchen. Beckett was spoon-deep in oatmeal, wearing the #27 jersey he'd slept in. Glitter from the poster still dotted his hair. "Morning, Flip-Flops," he said in Trace's exact inflection. Mae arched her brow. "Mockery before sunrise? Bold choice." Before he could fire back, a knock rattled the front door. Beckett's spoon clattered. "He's here! He's here!" Mae's heart did that stupid trampoline thing again. She tightened the belt of her robe and opened the door.

Trace stood on the porch, sun at his back, holding two to-go cups and a bakery box big enough to house a sheet cake. "Thought you could use breakfast," he said. "And maybe an ego boost." He lifted a thick envelope—inside, Mae glimpsed glossy photos: last night's victory shot with her and Beckett framed perfectly over Trace's shoulder. Her throat went tight. "You didn't have to—" "I wanted to," he said simply. Beckett bulldozed past her, hugging Trace at thigh-level. "Is that a maple bar? Please tell me that's a maple bar." Trace grinned. "Eat up, champ. I need your mom to come watch practice, and nobody supervises a track on an empty stomach." Mae's coffee-deprived brain lagged. "Practice? It's Monday." "Exactly. I run heat laps on the coast track every Monday. Thought you two might like the VIP view—plus, I owe you real dirt-side seats." Beckett was already stuffing his shoes on. Mae glanced down at her robe. "I need ten minutes." Trace's eyes flicked over her—robe, messy bun, bare legs—and lingered with unmistakable heat. "Take twelve. I'm enjoying the view."

The coast track sat on a cliffside lot just north of town—sand-packed straights, wooden berms, a view of the ocean that made every jump look like flight. Mae pressed her palms to the railing of the private platform while Beckett rattled off lap times into his phone. Trace ripped across the course with half a dozen other riders, but he was unmistakable—leaner in turns, higher in airtime, red gear a comet streaking against blue sky. Every pass sent a chill up her spine. She wasn't sure if it was fear or thrill—maybe both. During a pause, Trace idled below the platform, visor up. "You good?" he shouted. Mae gave a shaky thumbs-up. Beckett cupped his hands like a megaphone. "You're at thirty-eight-seven! Pick it up!" Trace laughed, saluted, and shot off again. The wind off the water whipped Mae's hair into her eyes; she pushed it back with sandy fingers and realized she was smiling—wide, unguarded, alive.

Practice wrapped before noon. Riders peeled off helmets, engines cooled, and someone cranked a portable speaker spilling 2000s punk over the pits. Trace jogged up the steps to the platform, shirt gone and torso glistening with honest sweat. Mae swallowed the utterly inappropriate sound her brain wanted to make. "Kid Jagger's a brutal coach," he said, ruffling Beckett's hair. "Keeps me humble." Beckett puffed his chest. "Someone's gotta." Trace turned to Mae, serious now. "Walk with me?" She nodded, and they made their way along the cliff path while Beckett stayed with a mechanic, happily cataloging tire compounds. Seagulls wheeled overhead. Waves smashed the rocks below. Trace kicked at a clump of sea grass. "Yesterday felt like more than a win." Mae hugged her arms against the breeze. "It was a great race."

He stopped, forcing her to face him. "It was a great *day*. You and Beckett—felt like something I didn't know I was missing until it was right in front of me." Mae's heartbeat skittered. The logical part of her wanted to correct him, to remind him this was temporary. But her tired, hopeful heart wanted to hear him say it again. "So," he continued, voice low, "I figure we've got two options. One: keep pretending this is casual and hope it doesn't kill me. Two: see where the hell this goes and risk everything." Mae's mouth was dry. "Everything?" He stepped closer, boots crunching gravel. "Yeah. Sponsors hate distractions. My schedule's insane. Your life's here, mine's everywhere. It's a terrible idea." "Sounds accurate." He brushed a knuckle down her arm. "Still want to try?" Her inhale shook. "I'm terrified." "Me too. Doesn't change how bad I want you." Silence fell, broken only by the ocean's roar. Then Mae reached up, grabbed his collar, and kissed him until the gulls got bored and flew elsewhere.

Trace's hands framed her face, thumbs stroking her cheekbones with a tenderness that contradicted the heat of his mouth. Mae slid her fingers into his hair—damp, salty, soft—and tugged just enough to feel him groan. He broke the kiss, breath ragged. "If we keep this up, I'm not letting you leave today." Mae's pulse stuttered. "Who says I'm leaving?" A wicked grin. "There's a tide pool cove down that trail. Private enough." Her brain screamed reasons to say no—Beckett, public indecency, sand in questionable places—but her body was already answering yes. They slipped down a narrow path, laughter tangled with crashing surf. The cove was a half-moon pocket of rock and moss, shielded from view. Trace kicked off boots; Mae ditched her sandals. The sand was cool, the water lapping at their ankles. He kissed her again, deeper now, hands finding the hem of her tank top. "Tell me to stop," he murmured. She arched into him. "Don't you dare." The top came off. The sea breeze kissed her skin. Trace swallowed a curse, eyes dark. He ran warm hands over her ribs, thumbs brushing the underside of her bra. Mae's breath hitched. Her fingers traced the ridge of his abs, following a scar along his side. "Bike vs. fence," he said. "Fence lose?" "Mostly." He unhooked her bra; it fell, caught by the breeze. His mouth followed, kissing over salt-slick skin, tongue drawing circles that made her toes curl in the sand. She tugged at his waistband. He laughed against her chest. "Eager?" "Shut up." He obliged, shedding joggers, leaving them both in minimal barriers. The ocean hissed in approval.

Trace backed her against a sun-warmed rock, kissed down her stomach, then lifted her in one fluid motion. She wrapped legs around his waist, the rock at her back, his body everywhere else. The world narrowed to heat, salt, and the muffled crash of waves. He entered her slowly, reverently, a stretch that drew a gasp from her throat. His forehead pressed to hers. "Okay?" "Better," she breathed. He moved—hips rolling, steady and deep. Mae clung, nails digging into his shoulders, pulse drumming in her ears. Every thrust was a promise, every moan swallowed by his mouth. The tide licked their feet, cool juxtaposition to the fire building between them. Mae's climax crept up like a rip current—sudden, unstoppable. She broke, cry muffled against his neck. Trace followed with a low growl, shuddering, holding her tight. They stayed like that, breathing each other, until reality slid back in on the tide. Trace eased her down, kissed her temple. "Still terrified?" She laughed, shaky and bright. "Terrified. And alive." He tucked a strand of hair behind her ear. "Good. Means we're doing it right."

They retrieved scattered clothes, laughing at sand in impossible places. Back at the pit, Beckett was still chattering at a mechanic, completely oblivious. On the drive home, Beckett regaled them with facts about two-stroke engines. Mae's hand sat on Trace's thigh, thumb tracing lazy patterns. At her curb, Trace killed the engine. Beckett bounded inside with leftover fries. Mae lingered. "When's your next race?" "Three weeks. Nevada." "Far." Trace caught her chin. "Distance is logistics. This—" he kissed her, slow and sure "—is the priority." She nodded, believing him more than she probably should. He pulled back. "I'll call tonight." Mae slipped out of the Bronco. "I'll answer." She watched him drive off, dust rising behind the tires, heart thumping like a restart gate. For the first time in a long time, she hoped the race never ended.

Chapter 10

Throttle The Curve

Mae woke up to a text.

Trace: *Still thinking about last night. Also thinking about you in my hoodie again. Also pancakes.*

She rolled onto her back, grinning like she was sixteen and freshly kissed. Beckett was already awake, judging by the faint sounds of cereal crunching and Minecraft commentary echoing down the hall. Her legs were still sore in a way she refused to regret. Her lips still tingled from Trace's kiss at the cove. And her heart? Her heart had apparently started practicing gymnastics without her consent. She should've felt terrified. This wasn't what she did—get swept up. Get soft. Get caught. But she wasn't terrified. She was hungry. For pancakes, yes. But also more. She texted back.

Mae: *If pancakes come with a side of answers, I'm in.*

Trace: *Answers are overrated. But my pancakes slap.*

They met at a tiny diner off Highway 9. The kind with cracked vinyl booths, syrup-sticky menus, and waitresses who called everyone "hon." Mae slid into the booth across from him, freshly showered and wearing sunglasses to mask the fact she hadn't slept more than four hours. Because her brain wouldn't shut up. Because she'd replayed every look, every kiss, every flicker of something real between them like it was a mixtape on repeat. Trace wore a grey Henley that made her want to cancel her whole day. His smile was easy, but his eyes—his eyes were searching. "Morning, Flip-Flops." "Morning, Pancake Daddy." He choked on his orange juice.

The waitress raised an eyebrow as she set down a carafe of coffee. "Y'all want cream, sugar, or just sexual tension?" Trace recovered with a grin. "Straight up, thanks." Mae added cream. And a little sass. "So what's the plan today? More covert kissing? Maybe a ride-along?" "Actually…" He reached into his jacket pocket and slid something across the table. Two all-access lanyards. Mae blinked. "You trying to seduce me with credentials?" "Is it working?" She stared at the pass, then at him. "What's the catch?" "No catch. Just want you there. Got a track demo later. Some new tech for the press. Figured you and Beckett might want to see what I look like covered in sweat and success." Mae narrowed her eyes. "I already saw you covered in both. Up close." Trace's smirk darkened. "Yeah. You did."

The track demo was held at a coastal training compound, complete with cliffs, curves, and a grandstand overlooking the ocean. Beckett practically combusted on sight. Trace introduced them to the team, handed Beckett a headset, and showed Mae the VIP tent. It wasn't fancy—just shade, snacks, and fans. But it came with one hell of a view. Trace mounted his bike and took off, all torque and elegance and danger.

Mae watched, transfixed. Every move was precise. Powerful. Like his body spoke the language of dirt and gravity. Like the wind belonged to him. Beckett gave commentary, but Mae couldn't focus on the words. Her eyes followed Trace's every curve. Every jump. Every near-impossible stunt.

And then— A sharp turn. Too sharp. His back tire caught a patch of loose gravel, and the bike wobbled. Time slowed. Trace leaned too hard. The front wheel buckled. The bike skidded sideways, and Trace was thrown. Mae screamed. Beckett ripped off the headset. "What happened?! MOM?!" Trace landed hard, rolling once, then twice, before coming to a stop. For a moment, everything stopped with him. Mae was already running.

By the time she reached him, two medics were already kneeling at his side. He was conscious. Breathing. Cursing. "Stupid gravel... nothing's broken... dammit, I told them to patch that curve..." Mae dropped to her knees beside him. "You okay?" she asked, breathless, eyes wild. Trace looked up, tried to smirk, but winced. "You came running. That's gotta mean something." She wanted to throttle him. Or kiss him. Maybe both. "You scared the hell out of me." "Wasn't on purpose." The medic cleared his throat. "Possible sprain. Maybe a rib. He needs to sit still." "Good luck with that," Mae muttered. Trace winced again. "You staying?" She nodded. "Obviously."

Back at the medic tent, Trace was patched up and pumped with electrolytes. Mae sat beside him, Beckett pacing with the kind of nervous energy only kids and caffeine can produce. "You gonna let me sign your cast?" Beckett asked hopefully. "No cast," Trace said. "But you can draw on my brace." "Deal." Mae handed Beckett her phone and turned to Trace. "You need to rest." "I'd rather flirt." "I'd rather not plan your funeral." He sobered slightly. "I'm fine. Really." "Yeah, well, you're not allowed to crash near cliffs anymore. Or at all. New rule." Trace reached out, his fingers brushing hers. "You were scared." Mae didn't answer. Just laced their fingers together.

That night, they ended up back at her place. Beckett crashed early, worn out from adrenaline and sun. Trace was quiet. Too quiet. Mae handed him an ice pack and sat beside him on the couch. "Talk to me," she said. "I hate sitting still." "I hate watching you almost die." He looked at her then. Really looked. "That's the thing, Mae. I didn't care about crashing before. Not like this. Not until there was something I didn't want to lose." Her heart flipped. Tripped. Freefell. "Trace…" "I like you. More than I should. More than makes sense for two weeks." "Same," she whispered. Silence stretched. Then Trace leaned in.

This kiss wasn't hungry. It wasn't rushed. It was gentle, unguarded—a kiss that felt like memory and possibility tangled together. His lips moved over hers with reverence, like he was imprinting her into the place behind his ribs. It was a promise. A prayer. A problem. Because neither of them wanted to say goodbye. And both knew goodbye was coming. When he pulled back, he didn't move far. His forehead rested against hers, breath warm, quiet between them. "I'm in deep," he said, voice low. Mae nodded, voice caught in her throat. "I know." Trace touched her cheek, eyes steady. "You make it hard to want anything else." "I was doing fine before you." "Same." A beat passed. Then he smiled softly, almost shyly. "But I'd still pick this. Even if it wrecks me." Mae kissed him again. Because she knew exactly what he meant.

Chapter 11

Pancake Promises and Pitfalls

The next morning arrived with a chorus of birds, the hum of Beckett's cartoons, and the distinct ache in Mae's chest that came with wanting something she couldn't keep. Trace was still asleep on her couch. She padded into the living room quietly, barefoot and disoriented, hair an honest disaster. Trace lay half-curled under the throw blanket, one arm bent behind his head, the other slung across his torso like he was casually modeling vulnerability. Mae froze in the doorway. Because seeing him there—so real, so domestic, so perfectly out of place in her world—wasn't fair. He was a man with dirt on his boots and crowds in his name. And she was just… Mae. But God, he looked good asleep. Like someone who hadn't had peace in a while. She tiptoed past him to the kitchen and started a pot of coffee, trying not to imagine what two weeks of this would do to her sanity—or her heart. "Morning," came a gravel-soft voice behind her. She jumped slightly. Turned.

Trace stood in the doorway, shirtless, eyes sleep-heavy, smile lazy. He looked like temptation served with syrup. "Jesus," she muttered, grabbing a mug. "You can't just sneak up on people looking like that."

"Sorry. Want me to put on a shirt?" "No. I mean—whatever. Your body, your rules." He crossed the kitchen in three barefoot steps and plucked a piece of toast from the rack. "You always this charming before caffeine?" She sipped from her mug, deadpan. "You're lucky I'm even speaking in full sentences." Trace leaned against the counter, chewing. "What's your day look like?" Mae shrugged. "Same as always. Drop Beckett at a playdate. Run errands. Resist the urge to emotionally spiral. You?" "Physical therapy check-in. Media calls. Pretending I'm not into a girl who makes fun of my playlist." "Pretend harder," she quipped. He laughed and stepped closer. "You make it hard." "Flatter me again and I might kiss you in front of the blender." "Promise?" She rolled her eyes, but her smile betrayed her. He reached for the coffee pot. "I'll pour the second cup. Don't want to risk you kissing me before I'm fully caffeinated."

They stood side by side, close enough to brush elbows, saying nothing and everything in the silence. For a brief second, it felt like a scene from a life Mae had never let herself dream about. They ate breakfast—pancakes and leftover strawberries and eggs Trace insisted on scrambling. He wasn't bad. He even flipped them with flair, tossing her a wink every time she tried to take over. "You know," she said between bites, "you're a menace in the kitchen." "Compliment noted." "Not a compliment." "Still noted." They were like that all morning—banter layered over glances that lingered too long.

Later that afternoon, Mae dropped Beckett off with his best friend for a playdate. The house was too quiet when she returned. No cartoon theme songs, no sound of toy car crashes. Just space. And silence. And the echo of Trace's laugh in her memory. It felt dangerous. So she cleaned. Not because the house needed it, but because she needed the illusion of control. She wiped counters that were already spotless. Vacuumed carpet that hadn't seen a footprint in hours. Scrubbed a pan that had only hosted water. Rearranged the spice rack alphabetically. Debated repainting the hallway. Then actually pulled out the paint samples. Every task was a stall tactic. Every chore was a way to delay thinking about how badly she wanted to see him again—how much she was already missing him. Halfway through reorganizing the junk drawer, her phone buzzed.

Trace: *Dinner tonight? My place. No cameras. No press. Just us.*

Mae stared at the screen, thumb hovering.

This wasn't a fling anymore. This wasn't just pancakes and kisses and adrenaline. This was real.

She typed back.

Mae: *I'll bring dessert. But if you expect me to wear heels, you're dreaming.*

Trace: *Flip-flops or nothing. Either way, I'll be distracted.*

She groaned and tossed the phone on the bed. Then flopped back beside it, staring at the ceiling. She hadn't felt like this since high school. Scratch that. Even her high school crush hadn't made her this dizzy. This, alive. This, completely, recklessly vulnerable. It was a little terrifying.

She went to the closet and pulled out something casual—a soft tee that clung just right and a pair of denim shorts that made her legs look longer than she felt. She dug around for her favorite earrings. Spritzed perfume. Then changed her shirt. Twice. Brushed her teeth. Applied mascara, washed it off, applied it again. Debated whether lip gloss made her look like she was trying too hard. By the time she walked out the door, she was practically buzzing. And if her stomach did a little somersault every time she thought about his smile—well, that was no one's business but hers.

She drove to the store, grabbed a pint of the overpriced gelato she only bought when she was spiraling, then stared at the wine aisle for ten minutes like it held the secrets to the universe. Finally, she picked a red with a decent label and no screw cap. Because if she was going to fall into something reckless, she was at least going to be classy about it. She was in trouble. Big, delicious, unforgivable trouble. And for the first time in a long time, she didn't want to be saved from it.

Chapter 12

Dinner & Other Dangerous Things

Trace lived in a gated rental just off the cliffs—one of those places with ocean views and a driveway long enough to question your tax bracket. Mae parked at the bottom and took a deep breath before walking up. The front door opened before she even knocked. "Thought I heard your car," Trace said, leaning against the doorframe in joggers and a T-shirt that looked criminally good. "You came." Mae held up the wine and gelato. "I bribe well." He grinned and stepped aside. "Come on in."

The house was cozy but modern. Surfboards leaned in the corners like art pieces. Framed photos of dirt bikes and finish lines dotted the walls. But there were softer touches too—candles, mismatched throw pillows, a blanket draped across the back of the couch like someone actually used it. "Nice place. Didn't peg you for the decorative throw kind." "It came with the rental," he said. "But I've grown attached." He took the wine and gelato, setting them on the kitchen island. The air smelled like garlic and butter and something slightly burnt. Mae wrinkled her nose. "You cooked?" "Attempted," he admitted. "Backup plan's in the freezer if you hate it."

She peered into the skillet, inspecting its contents with the wariness of a bomb technician. Shrimp, linguine, a suspicious amount of garlic. A few rogue pieces of parsley clung to the edges. "What exactly is this?" "Shrimp linguine. Possibly poison. You've been warned." She laughed. "I've eaten chicken nuggets off a Batman plate. My standards are subterranean." "Perfect. I specialize in 'barely edible but charming.'" He plated their food, handing hers over with a flourish and a wink. They walked out to the balcony, where the sky was caught between golden hour and early dusk, streaked with hues that made Mae's chest feel oddly light.

They sat with their legs kicked up on the railing, plates balanced on their laps, shoulders bumping occasionally. Below them, the ocean sighed against the cliffs in slow, hypnotic rhythm. The salt air mingled with the scent of garlic and something slightly overcooked—but she didn't mind. Trace took a bite and winced. "Okay, I'm officially downgrading this to 'edible if you're already emotionally attached to me.'" Mae chewed, swallowed, and grinned. "Lucky for you, I'm a sucker for effort and dangerous smiles." "You just admitted I'm dangerous. Noted." "Dangerously *adjacent*." He laughed, and it wasn't loud or dramatic—it was warm. Low. The kind of laugh that seeps under your skin and stays there. "So," she said between bites. "What's it like being famous and hiding in rental houses?"

Trace shrugged. "Weird. Fun. Lonely, sometimes. People think they know you because they've seen you do flips on a bike. But they don't know what your mom said to you on graduation day. Or what song wrecks you. Or how you take your coffee." "Black, two sugars." He looked over. "You remembered." "I have a weird brain." "I like your weird brain." She rolled her eyes. "Smooth." "Honest." They finished the meal with gelato straight from the carton, passing it back and forth. A playlist hummed from the living room—bluesy rock, something old and full of feeling.

Eventually, Trace stood and offered his hand. "Come here." "Why? You gonna dance around the kitchen?" "Maybe." He did. Barefoot and off-rhythm, they swayed between the island and the sink, her head on his chest, his hand pressed to the small of her back. The music was slow, their bodies slower. Every touch buzzed like a live wire. "This is dangerous," Mae whispered. "You scared?" "Terrified." "Good. Me too." The kiss started soft. Familiar. Like a sentence they'd both been finishing in their heads. But it deepened—hands in hair, fingers gripping fabric, mouths finding rhythm. He lifted her onto the counter, kissed her like it was the first and last time, and for a moment, nothing existed but heat and heartbeats. She tugged his shirt over his head. He peeled hers off just as gently. Skin met skin, and everything between them sparked alive. Trace traced his mouth down the curve of her neck, whispering something low and reverent. She wrapped her legs around his waist, pulling him closer, feeling every ounce of tension unravel. They didn't make it to the bedroom.

The counter. The couch. The soft rug beneath the coffee table. Each touch built on the last—frantic, aching, beautiful. Laughter broke through the urgency more than once. So did whispering her name like a secret. Trace's fingers tangled in her hair as her back arched under his mouth. She gasped his name, hands pressed to his shoulder blades like she was holding herself to earth. When she rolled him over on the rug, grinning like the rule-breaker she'd always been, he let her take the lead. And then, when she was breathless and wrecked above him, he flipped her gently, slowly, reverently—as if memorizing the way her body bowed for him. They rediscovered each other over and over again—slower the second time, quieter the third. At some point, the music stopped, but neither of them noticed. Time stretched and folded. When they finally collapsed on the couch, tangled and breathless, she laughed again. "What?" he asked, brushing hair from her face. "I'm wearing your hoodie again." He smiled, leaning down to kiss her forehead. "That's not an accident."

Later, curled up on the couch with her legs in his lap, Mae realized something terrifying: She hadn't thought about the exit strategy. She didn't want one. And Trace Jagger? He looked like a man with no intention of leaving easy. They stayed like that for a while. The gelato melted in its carton, the playlist looped without them noticing, and the moon rose high above the cliffs. Trace absentmindedly traced circles on her thigh with the pad of his thumb. Every once in a while, he'd glance down at her like he was still making sure she was real. "What happens after this?" she finally asked, her voice low. "After dessert or after us?" She tilted her head up to look at him. "You tell me." Trace let out a breath, leaned his head back against the couch. "I don't know. I leave in five days. I've got tour stops, appearances, the usual chaos. But this? You? I didn't plan for this." "Yeah," Mae said quietly. "Me neither."

Silence fell again, but it wasn't heavy—it was thoughtful. Tense in a way that made her wonder how quickly good things could start to feel dangerous. Finally, he looked back down at her. "Come with me." Mae blinked. "What?" "Just for the weekend. My next stop's only two hours from here. It's low-key. More exhibitions than competition. Beckett could come. You'd both have fun. And I'd get more time with you." Her stomach did something deeply inconvenient. "Are you seriously inviting me to hit the road with a dirt bike legend?" "No," he said. "I'm inviting you to spend more time with the guy who makes you coffee and listens to your weird playlists. The motocross legend's just a bonus." She stared at him, emotions bubbling so fast she couldn't grab onto one. "I'll think about it," she said. He smiled. "Fair. But I'm not above bribing you." "Oh, I know. That hoodie's a whole strategy." "Caught me." She kissed him once more—just once, slow and aching—and leaned her head on his shoulder. It was dangerous. And completely worth it.

Chapter 13

Too Perfect, Too Soon

The morning after was suspiciously perfect. Mae woke up tucked beneath a throw blanket, her legs stretched across Trace's lap, the early sunlight just beginning to sneak through the windows. Trace was already awake, one hand lazily tracing circles on her knee, his other scrolling through something on his phone. He looked relaxed. Unbothered. Dangerous in that quiet, domestic way that made her chest ache. "You stare in your sleep," he said, eyes still on his screen. She snorted. "You talk like you've had multiple nights of data." "One night. Four observations. A running hypothesis." "Which is?" "You dream about carbs and chaos." She laughed, but it caught in her throat. Because it wasn't just funny. It was intimate. It felt too close. Too… real. "You hungry?" he asked, setting his phone aside. "Starving. But if you tell me you cook breakfast the same way you cook dinner—" "I make a mean waffle," he cut in. "And I didn't even burn the bacon last time. Only mildly singed."

Mae stretched, reluctantly pulling herself upright. "Waffles sound dangerously close to commitment." He stood, offering a hand. "Then it's a good thing I've got commitment issues." She rolled her eyes and followed him into the kitchen, trying not to notice how easily they fit in each other's rhythm. He pulled out ingredients while she made coffee. Their movements overlapped, brushing shoulders, sharing glances, bumping hips. Easy. Too easy. "Why do you even own a waffle iron?" she asked, watching him stir batter like a man who'd definitely Googled it first. "It was a gift. From a fan. With a note that said, 'Fuel like a champ.'" She arched a brow. "Please tell me that wasn't a euphemism." "I'm not sure. The card had glitter." Mae laughed, stepping around him to pour two mugs of coffee. Trace leaned in and kissed her temple before she could react—soft and casual, like it was the most natural thing in the world. And maybe that was the problem. Everything about him was starting to feel natural. By the time they sat down with syrup-drenched waffles and mugs of coffee, Mae was spiraling internally. She wasn't supposed to like him this much. He wasn't supposed to make her feel this safe. And she definitely wasn't supposed to picture what mornings like this might look like on a regular basis.

She took a deep breath, shoved another bite into her mouth, and forced herself to be present. "What's your plan after the race season?" she asked casually. Trace shrugged. "Not sure yet. Maybe a break. My body's been screaming at me for years. A couple months off wouldn't hurt. Maybe visit my sister in Oregon. Catch up on sleep. Get bored." "You have a sister?" "You sound shocked." "You just don't give off 'family barbecue' energy." "Well, she's the only person who ever beat me in a go-kart race, so I try to forget." Mae grinned, sipping her coffee. "Older or younger?" "Older. By four years. She's the brainiac. Engineer. Got me into racing, actually. Built my first dirt bike out of spare parts and stubbornness." Mae blinked. "That's...kind of incredible."

Trace smiled, his expression softening in a way that made her stomach twist. "Yeah. She's amazing. Doesn't take any crap from anyone either. Reminds me of someone." "Careful, Jagger. I might blush." "Wouldn't be the worst thing." She rolled her eyes, but the smile lingered. It was getting harder and harder to keep her walls up. Every moment with him chipped away at them—effortlessly, relentlessly. And the scary part? She wasn't sure she wanted to stop it.

They cleaned up together, trading insults and dish soap flicks. He chased her around the kitchen with a wet sponge until she threatened to dump the entire coffee pot down his joggers. Then, laughing and breathless, they collapsed onto the couch again. Mae curled into the corner, Trace beside her, both quiet for a moment as the morning sun climbed higher. "You ever think about what it would be like to just... disappear for a while?" he asked, voice low. She looked over. "Like off-grid? Or faking your death and starting a new life in Canada?" "Somewhere in between." She nodded. "All the time." "What stops you?" Mae looked down at her hands. Thought about Beckett. About the life she'd built from scratch. About the fear of what letting go might cost her. "Reality," she said finally. "And my kid. And the fact that I'm really bad at surviving without Wi-Fi." Trace chuckled. "That last one would do it." Another quiet pause.

Then he shifted closer, brushing her hair behind her ear. "You scare the hell out of me." "Good. Because you terrify me." He smiled, and then he kissed her again—slow, deliberate. Like he wasn't afraid of the consequences. Mae let herself fall into it, just for a second. Let herself imagine what it would be like if he wasn't leaving in a few days. If this wasn't temporary. If her heart wasn't already tangled up in something that had no business feeling like forever. But when he pulled back, she said nothing. Just leaned her head on his shoulder and closed her eyes, pretending the clock wasn't ticking. Because for now, it was perfect. Even if it was a little too perfect.

CHAPTER 14

Reality Check, Party Of One

Mae woke up to the sound of her phone vibrating violently on the nightstand, a migraine waiting to happen. She squinted at the screen: 7:04 a.m., six missed texts, two from her sister, one from Beckett's best friend's mom, and three from Beckett himself. The most recent read: **"MOM. Trace Jagger is on the cover of MOTOWEEKLY. AND HE TALKED ABOUT YOU."** Mae sat straight up. Coffee. She needed coffee, a helmet, and maybe someone to talk her out of spiraling.

Ten minutes later, she had half a cup of caffeine in her veins and was doom-scrolling. There it was—Trace Jagger on the cover of *MotoWeekly*, helmet in hand, grin cocky as hell. Below his smolder: **"Trace Jagger Talks Retirement, Romance, and What Comes Next."** "No, no, no," Mae muttered, clicking through. There, in the second paragraph: **"She's smart, sarcastic, strong as hell. She tackled me in flip-flops. I think I fell for her before I hit the ground."** Mae closed the article and stared at her kitchen wall for a full five minutes. She'd been trying—very hard—not to fall. And here he was, falling publicly.

By noon, Beckett was home, buzzing with excitement. He wore his #TeamTrace hoodie and carried a signed race flag that Trace must've dropped off at some ungodly hour. "So... you and Trace are, like, a thing? Like a real thing?" Mae blinked. "What makes you say that?" "He said 'romance.' That's not just friends who high-five. That's kissing." She sighed. "Can we not talk about kissing right now?" Beckett tilted his head. "Do you like him?" Mae opened her mouth. Closed it. "Yes." Beckett grinned. "Cool. I like him too. I mean, not like that. Ew. But like... I'd be fine if he stuck around."

That night, Mae stood on her porch, phone in hand, trying to draft a text. Something casual. Something that didn't sound like she was in too deep. Something that didn't hint she'd read every word of the article three times. She didn't send anything. Instead, Trace showed up. He pulled up in the Bronco, headlights washing across her lawn. She stepped outside, heart slamming like it had something to prove. He got out slowly, watching her. "You saw it." Mae nodded. "You talked about me in an international magazine." "I meant every word." She crossed her arms. "You didn't ask." "Because if I'd asked, you would've told me no." She didn't respond. "I'm not trying to blow up your life, Mae. But I'm not trying to be forgettable either." He stepped closer. "I want this. I want you. And if that means adjusting my life, I will. I've done the fame thing. I've done the grind. I want something real." She looked at him—really looked. The man who kissed her like a prayer, who danced barefoot in his kitchen, who learned how she took her coffee without asking. And just like that, her carefully stacked defenses gave out. She stepped into him. And didn't let go.

They spent the evening curled on the couch, a movie playing in the background—some half-forgotten action flick with explosions that shook the speakers every five minutes. Mae's head rested in the crook of Trace's shoulder while his fingertips traced idle patterns along her thigh: lazy circles, figure-eights that drifted higher whenever the plot went quiet. Each touch was a silent admission—*I like you too much to stop touching you.* Mae tried to follow the storyline, but her mind looped on dangerous thoughts: how perfectly his laugh fit in her living room, how easily her son trusted him, how terrifying it felt to miss him when he was still right there. She was half in love with a man who'd once made headlines for body-slamming another racer and now made headlines for quoting romantic nonsense about her in major magazines. The duality made her dizzy. " You ever think you're bad at this?" she asked, eyes still on the screen's flickering light. "Relationships? Constantly," he answered without missing a beat. "But I think you're worth figuring it out for." The words landed with a softness that stole her breath. She lifted an eyebrow, smirking. "Damn. That's good. Did you practice that?" "Three mirrors and a motivational playlist."

Mae snorted a laugh into his shoulder, and the vibration of her amusement traveled into his chest. Trace kissed the top of her head, lingering. For a suspended moment the world shrank to the quiet hum of the TV, the steady beat of his heart under her ear, and the citrus-and-sawdust scent that clung to his hoodie. Maybe—just for tonight—nothing was about to go wrong. The bills, the distance, the press vultures, the knowledge that he'd be on a flight in four days—all of it faded beneath the comforting weight of his arm. She tilted her face up, catching his gaze. In the low light his eyes looked almost copper, reflecting the TV fireball currently demolishing a fictional city. "You know I'm scared out of my mind, right?" Trace nodded once. "Me too. Difference is, I'm done running from things that scare me. Racing taught me that the fastest way out of a turn is to lean in." Mae swallowed, feeling the metaphor lodge somewhere beneath her ribs. "Lean in, huh?" "Full throttle, Flip-Flops." His grin was soft, but his voice was steel. She kissed him—slow, tasting salt from popcorn and something sweeter underneath. When she pulled back, she whispered, "Don't make promises you can't keep." "Wouldn't dare," he murmured, thumb brushing her lower lip.

Outside, wind rattled the windows—a coastal gust that sounded too much like a warning. Because they both knew this wasn't a fairytale. There were contracts to sign, cameras to dodge, ex-husbands who still called about child-support adjustments. Consequences. People watching. Expectations sharpening their knives. Some storm was coming. PR fallout, paparazzi ambush, or maybe just the brutal ticking of a countdown clock until Trace's departure. They just didn't know when. So they did what reckless, hopeful people do on the edge of a forecast—they held each other tighter, hearts synchronic in the flicker of TV light, and pretended the thunder was still a long way off.

Chapter 15

Headlines and Headaches

Trace left early the next morning for a team meeting—something about suspension tweaks and an interview scheduled for noon. He stood at the door longer than he needed to, one hand cradling her cheek, the other tangled gently in her hair. He kissed her like he didn't want to leave, like the hours without her were already too many. "I'll text when I'm done," he said against her lips. "I'll be here," she murmured, but it came out softer than she meant. He hesitated, gave her that crooked smile she was beginning to recognize as his tells-everything-and-nothing look, and finally walked out the door. Mae tried to act casual about it. She padded barefoot into the kitchen and poured herself a coffee. The morning light streamed through the windows in buttery gold, too bright for how off-kilter she suddenly felt. She responded to emails she barely read. Double-checked Beckett's school reminder. Replied to a group text from Tori with a thumbs up she didn't mean. And still, every few minutes, her eyes flicked toward the front door like he might come back. She ignored the twitch in her chest like her heart missed him on instinct. Like her body already noticed the absence before her brain could catch up. By 11 a.m., her phone started blowing up.

Group Text: BESTIES WHO WILL BURY BODIES FOR YOU

Tori: *Girl. You need to sit down.*

Mae: *Why?? I'm fine??*

Tori: *You're not. Google Trace Jagger + Red Dress.*

Her stomach dropped. She opened her browser.

And there it was.

Motocross Heartthrob Trace Jagger Spotted With Mystery Woman in Red—Sources Say It's Serious

Below the headline was a blurry but undeniable photo: Trace, arm slung around her shoulders, both of them laughing as they exited the gelato shop. Her red sundress was unmistakable. So was his grin. Mae's stomach flipped. It shouldn't have mattered. But it did. Not because it was a bad photo. Not because the internet knew. But because now it *wasn't* just theirs. Now it was everyone's. Another ping.

Tori: *You're officially tabloid famous. Want me to call your ex and gloat?*

Mae: *Please do.*

She wasn't mad. Not exactly. But she also wasn't ready to be someone's headline. Her life had always been hers—messy, private, quiet in all the ways it had to be. And suddenly, she was trending. Not because of a project. Not because of Beckett. Because of Trace. Her thoughts were still chasing themselves when the front door opened. Trace. Back early. Holding two smoothies and wearing an expression that could go either direction—half amusement, half caution. "So... guess who's trending?" Mae arched an eyebrow. "Was it the dress? Or the glitter on Beckett's sign?" "Your legs," he said without missing a beat, crossing the room to kiss her. "Also your smile. Apparently, it's dangerous." "Good. Maybe it'll keep the trolls from commenting on your taste in women."

He handed her a smoothie and looked her over like he was checking for bruises. "You okay?" She hesitated. "Not used to being... visible. It's weird." "Want me to say something to the press? Shut it down?" Mae shook her head, sipping slowly. "No. Just... don't ghost me and marry a pop star." Trace grinned, the tension in his shoulders easing. "Only if you promise not to get a TikTok deal for dating me." "Damn. There go my influencer dreams." They clinked smoothies. But even as they sipped, the air between them had shifted. Just a little. Not bad. Not scary. Just... real. Mae set her smoothie down and wrapped her arms around herself. "I'm not used to sharing things that matter. I'm used to control. Predictable chaos. Beckett's dentist appointments and PTA newsletters. You're...not that."

Trace walked over and pulled her gently into his chest. "I know. And I'm not asking you to give everything. Just—don't push me out before I have a chance to prove I'm worth staying." She looked up at him. "You planning to stay?" "I'm planning to try. If you'll let me." Mae didn't have a roadmap for this. But when she nodded, his hand slid up to cup her jaw, and he kissed her like the chaos was worth it. And for the first time, maybe she believed it too.

Chapter 16

The Away Game

Mae had never been a "travel for the weekend" kind of woman. Single mom life didn't exactly lend itself to impromptu escapes. But when Trace had texted her earlier in the week— *"Race weekend. Out of town. Want you there. Just you."*—something in her chest had lit up like a flare. She'd stared at the message for three full minutes before replying.

Mae: Are you asking me on a mini-vacation?

Trace: Only if you're into hotels with questionable carpeting and room service burritos. It's romantic as hell. Come with me.

Mae: What about Beckett?

Trace: I mean... I like the kid, but I was thinking something a little more adult this time.

Mae: You mean you want me. Alone. Overnight.

Trace: Unless that's terrifying.

Mae: Oh, it is. But I'm still in.

So now, Friday morning, she was standing in her hallway, trying to zip a duffel bag without breaking the zipper and simultaneously texting Tori.

Mae: You sure Beckett won't be too much?

Tori: He's bringing three bags of snacks and a controller. I won't even see him until Sunday night.

Mae: Call if he gets twitchy. Or if he eats all your cereal.

Tori: Go get laid, woman.

Mae snorted, shoved one more hoodie into the bag, and zipped it with a triumphant grunt.

Trace picked her up in a blacked-out truck that looked like it belonged in an action movie. The bed was filled with gear. His bike was strapped down like a prized stallion, gleaming under the morning sun. He leaned out the window and grinned. "This is the part where I say get in, loser, we're going racing." She laughed, tossing her bag into the cab. "You're lucky I packed extra underwear." He wiggled his brows. "For the racing, right?" She climbed in, smirking. "Keep dreaming, Jagger."

The drive was hours of easy banter and shared playlists. Trace drove like he rode—confident, focused, a little reckless around corners. Mae kept sneaking glances at his profile, the way his hands wrapped around the wheel, the occasional stretch of his neck when he sang along to old songs. Somewhere around the second hour, as the playlist cycled into nostalgic early 2000s alt-rock, Mae said, "Did you seriously make a mix that includes every angsty teen anthem known to man?" Trace chuckled. "Listen, Dashboard Confessional is sacred. Don't question the classics." "Oh, I'm not questioning. I'm judging. There's a difference." "Fine, Flip-Flops. What's your road trip song, then?" "Anything that lets me sing until my throat hurts and makes me forget I haven't had a real vacation in six years." "That narrows it down. Want to take the aux?" She grinned, reaching for his phone. "Prepare to be serenaded." They sang loud and off-key, harmonizing like drunk karaoke contestants, laughing between choruses. It felt reckless. It felt free.

Between verses, they talked about everything—his first race, her worst date, the one time she tried to make a Pinterest-worthy birthday cake and ended up with a frosting-covered kitchen disaster. "So you're saying domestic goddess isn't your vibe?" he asked. "I'm saying my vibe is more 'survival mode with sass.'" "Hot." She rolled her eyes. "You're easy to impress." "Not true," he said. "You're just that good." They stopped halfway for snacks—Mae returned to the truck with sour straws and a suspiciously neon sports drink. Trace handed her a greasy breakfast burrito he claimed was from a gas station run by saints. "Might kill you, might be divine," he said. "Fifty-fifty." She took a bite. Eyes widened. "Oh my God. This is heaven in tortilla form." He smirked. "Told you. I only poison people I don't like." "You're full of romance, you know that?" "Just wait until I show you the continental breakfast." By the time they reached the race compound, her cheeks hurt from smiling.

The hotel was... exactly what Trace promised. Slightly faded, vaguely floral curtains, but clean. The kind of place that smelled like Febreze and lukewarm ambition. Trace tossed his duffel on the bed. "Home sweet home." Mae flopped dramatically onto the mattress. "There better be a waffle maker in the lobby." "Oh, baby. There's a pancake robot. You're in for luxury." She laughed and kicked off her shoes. "Race first.

Waffles later." He leaned against the doorframe, watching her as she stretched across the bed. "You always make yourself at home this fast?" "Only when I'm with someone who makes the room feel safer than it looks." His eyes flickered. Softened. But he didn't say anything—just walked over and gently tugged her upright. "Come on. I wanna show you the track."

Race day was chaos in the best way. The crowd was smaller than the Redwood track, but just as intense. Fans lined the fences. Mechanics shouted into radios. Trace disappeared into the pit area while Mae found a decent spot near the front, VIP badge swinging from her lanyard. The roar of engines filled the air. Dust swirled like smoke. Mae wiped her sunglasses and tucked her hair behind her ears as announcers bellowed rider names through tinny speakers. When Trace emerged in full gear—blue and white this time—he scanned the crowd until he found her. He winked.

Mae's stomach did a barrel roll. He climbed onto his bike, revved the engine once, twice. The sound was pure electricity. The gate dropped. He launched like a shot, weaving through the opening stretch like it was muscle memory. Mae screamed his name, caught up in the chaos of cheering fans, adrenaline, and flying dirt. Each lap brought him closer, faster, more dialed in. Mae watched through fingers curled over the barrier, shouting every time he passed. He slid around corners with precision. Soared over jumps like his tires had wings. He was beautiful to watch. Terrifying too.

By the final lap, he'd carved a solid lead. Mae's voice cracked from yelling. Her chest ached like her heart was trying to keep pace with his. He crossed the finish line first. The crowd erupted. Mae burst into applause. She didn't care that her hands were dirty or her hair wind-tangled. He did it. He really did it. Trace lifted his helmet as he circled back toward the pit. Found her in the crowd. Pointed right at her and grinned like he'd just won the damn lottery. And in that second, Mae knew something had shifted. For real. He wasn't just showing off. He was racing for her. And worse? She wanted him to.

Chapter 17

Race Night

Trace was still riding high from the podium—gear half-unzipped, salt-slick hair falling over mischievous eyes, a grin that promised trouble. Cameras flashed, fans screamed, but Mae felt like he was the only thing in focus. When he found her through the chaos and crooked a single finger, heat pulsed low in her belly. **"Come here, Flip-Flops."** His voice—low, rough velvet—left no room for argument. She went. After the champagne, after the reporters, he led her behind the trailers, fingers wrapped around her wrist. Every purposeful stride screamed *mine.* They ducked into the team camper—dim lights, fuel musk, a bassline thumping from a party somewhere outside. The door snapped shut. **Click.**

Mae's back met the kitchenette counter; Trace's body caged hers in. One big palm settled at her throat—not squeezing, just claiming—while the other tugged her ponytail back so her mouth tipped up to him. "Been hard since lap one," he breathed against her lips. "Thinking about how you gasp when I tell you what to do." Her pulse stuttered. "Then tell me." "Good girl," he growled, kissing her hard—teeth, bite, tongue that took without apology. She opened willingly, moaning when he nipped her bottom lip. Hands roamed—his sliding under her hoodie to palm bare skin; hers clawing at the damp race shirt clinging to his torso. "Off," he ordered. She yanked the hoodie up; he ripped the tee overhead, tossing it aside. His gaze dragged over her bra, hunger sparking darker. "Look at you… fuck, I love this body." Heat flushed her chest. "Do something about it."

Trace's answering chuckle was sin. "On the couch. Knees up." She obeyed, scrambling onto the narrow sofa. His command settled like a weight—delicious, electric. She *liked* following when it was him. He knelt between her spread thighs, dragged her jeans off inch by torturous inch. Kissed the inside of her knee, then higher—pausing to bite the soft flesh till she whimpered. "Use your words, Mae." "Need your mouth," she panted. "Please." "That's it." He licked a stripe up her underwear, pressure firm, eyes locked on hers. "So polite. Keep begging." "Trace—please. Need you to make me come." "Louder." She repeated it, shameless now, and he rewarded her—tongue and lips working through fabric until she trembled. He pulled the panties aside, dove in with a groan. Dirty words spilled from his mouth between licks—how sweet she tasted, how wet she was for him, how she'd better not come until he said.

The command held her on a razor edge. When he finally growled, **"Now, let go,"** pleasure ripped through her, back arching off the couch. He rose, wiping his mouth with the back of his hand, eyes burning. "Turn over, hands on the cushion." Adrenaline crashed with want. She flipped, presenting, heartbeat roaring in her ears. The zipper of his pants rasped; a condom packet tore. One broad palm landed on her ass—**smack.** She gasped, heat flooding where the sting bloomed. "You love that," he murmured, lining up. "Say it." "I love it. Love your hands. Love—" He thrust in, seating deep in one stroke. Words dissolved into a broken cry.

"God, yes. Take it." His grip bruised her hips, pace slow torture. "So tight around me. Mine, huh?" "All yours," she moaned, pushing back to meet every drive. He fucked her in measured thrusts, praising and claiming between each—calling her *good girl, perfect pussy, my Mae.* Dirty, tender, dominant. She soaked up every filthy syllable.

Soon the rhythm snapped—harder, faster, his chest blanketing her back, hand sliding to her throat again. "Gonna come with me?" "Please—please." His teeth grazed her ear. "Do it. Make a mess on me." Pleasure detonated—she shattered, muscles clamping, a strangled scream swallowed by the cushions. Trace followed with a raw groan, thrusts jerking as he spilled into the condom. For long seconds they just breathed—sweaty, shaking, limbs tangled. He eased out, disposing of the condom, then scooped her into his lap sideways on the couch. Hoodie draped over them like a flag claimed. "You okay, gorgeous?" She managed a sated laugh. "Pretty sure I transcended." He kissed her sweaty temple. "Told you dashboards and drivel couldn't compete with us." She nuzzled into his neck, loving the dominance still humming in the way his arms locked around her. Safe and thrilling all at once. "Round two in the shower," he murmured. "I'm washing your hair. Then pinning you against the tile." Her answering smile was pure wicked. "Better set a lap record, champ. I recover fast."

Outside, engines quieted, parties faded, but inside the camper their night was just beginning—full of steam and sharp commands, worship and whispered filthy promises, until exhaustion finally stole them into tangled sleep. And Mae, drifting off with his heartbeat under her cheek, realized the scariest truth yet: She'd never felt so thoroughly, wildly... *wanted.*

Chapter 18

The Flashbulb

Sunday morning came too fast. Mae woke up tangled in a mess of sheets and sweat and limbs that weren't hers alone. Her body ached—in all the best ways—and she didn't dare move just yet. Trace was behind her, one arm wrapped firmly around her waist, the other tucked beneath her pillow. He breathed steady against her neck, the weight of him still grounding. For the first time in years, she didn't want to check her phone. But real life had a habit of barging in. A vibration buzzed somewhere in the pile of clothes on the floor. Trace grumbled but didn't move. Mae slid out of bed quietly and dug her phone from her jeans. One look at the screen made her stomach twist. *Incoming call: Tori.*

She answered on the third ring. "He's fine," Tori said without preamble. "But you might want to brace yourself." Mae blinked. "What happened?" "The internet happened. There are pics. Of you. Of Trace. Kissing. In the pit yesterday. Some fan posted a video and it blew up overnight." Mae's heart stuttered. "How bad?" "Not bad unless you hate going viral. People are obsessed. He's trending. You're trending. Beckett's poster is now on two meme pages. I mean... it's flattering. Ish. But also...

intense." Trace sat up in bed, rubbing his eyes. "Everything okay?" Mae covered the phone. "You're famous again. And apparently, I am too." He grinned, cocky and still half-asleep. "Was it the kiss or the ass grab?" "Trace," she hissed, face flaming. Tori was still talking. "Also? Some sports tabloid is running a headline like 'Throttle Problems: Is Motocross's Wildest Racer Finally Settling Down?' with your picture beside it." Mae groaned. "I hate everything." Trace wrapped an arm around her waist, pulling her back into bed. He kissed her shoulder, voice gravelly and smug. "I don't know. I kinda like the sound of that." "Of what?" "Settling down. With you."

She turned to face him, heart jackhammering against her ribs. "Trace…" "I know, I know. It's only been a few weeks. But it doesn't feel like it. I've never brought anyone into this part of my life before. Not like this. Not fully. And I don't want this to just be a chapter we look back on. I want more." The air went still. Mae swallowed. Her walls threatened to rise like floodgates, but she held them down. Just this once, she let herself feel it. Let herself believe it. "Okay," she said softly. "More." He leaned in and kissed her, slow and deep, like he had nowhere else to be. And for a while, neither of them moved. The world outside could spin, flashbulbs could pop, headlines could scream. Inside that hotel room, it was just them. And maybe, for once, the chaos was calm.

Later that morning, Trace texted his publicist. *We're not denying it.* Mae, wrapped in a hotel robe and sipping coffee on the balcony, caught sight of the message over his shoulder. Her brow arched. "That's bold." He turned slightly, eyes gleaming with something solid. Unshakable. "So am I," he said, winking. She shook her head, but her smile lingered.

The news had already hit every sports blog. Fans were reposting clips of Trace kissing her in the pit with dramatic captions like *#PowerCoupleGoals* and *ThrottleQueen*. It was surreal. Weird. A little terrifying. But when he handed her a second coffee, set it down beside her with a kiss to her temple, Mae felt...okay. Better than okay. Because maybe being bold wasn't so bad. Maybe it was exactly what they needed. She looked out at the morning sky, listened to the steady hum of traffic below, and leaned into him. "You sure about this?" she asked, voice quiet. "Mae," he said, brushing a thumb down her jaw, "I've never been more sure of anything." Her heart thudded like it recognized something true. Maybe, just maybe, they were ready for the next lap. And this time, they weren't racing alone.

Chapter 19

Twist Me, Don't Test Me

By Monday morning, Mae was back home, sitting on the edge of her bathtub, hair in a towel, staring at the open tabloid on her phone. Trace Jagger had officially entered her world—and not quietly. Photos of them at the race. The kiss. The hand on her lower back. Her legs crossed in that red sundress. All of it had been meme'd, captioned, dissected. And worse? She looked happy. "Freakin' fantastic," she muttered. Her phone buzzed again.

Trace: *Smile. You're trending.*

Mae: *I'm going to murder you with a glitter pen.*

Trace: *Kinky. What time should I be there?*

Mae laughed despite herself. She didn't want to like it. She didn't want to like any of this—the publicity, the fan theories, the weird Reddit threads claiming she was a motocross groupie with excellent legs. But damn it, she kind of did. By Wednesday, Trace was back in town. He picked her up in the Bronco, this time wearing sunglasses and a hat like it might keep him inconspicuous. It didn't. Dinner was somewhere nice, and dessert was... Well. Dessert was back at her place. They didn't even make it past the entryway.

Trace kicked the door closed behind him, pressing her back against it, his mouth already on hers. "You wore that dress on purpose," he growled against her neck. "I didn't even know you were coming over." He smirked, lifting her effortlessly. "Then your subconscious wants me just as bad." Mae wrapped her legs around him, arms tightening around his shoulders. "That's not news." He carried her to the couch, laying her out like something priceless. Hands sliding up her thighs, under the hem of the dress. "Do you have any idea what it did to me?" he murmured. "Seeing you in that red dress, all soft and snug while the world watched?" She arched into his touch. "Tell me." His voice dropped, dark and raw. "Made me want to take you right there. On the hood of the Bronco. Let them film that too." Mae moaned. "Yeah," he whispered. "You like that. You like being mine even when they all see." She pulled him down by the collar, mouth crashing into his. "I'm not yours." He smirked. "Not yet. But tonight? You will be." And then he showed her exactly what he meant.

Trace didn't rush. He peeled her out of the dress like he was unwrapping a secret meant only for him, fingers slow, mouth slower. He worshipped every inch—his hands firm, his lips hot, his voice a low current of filthy promises in her ear. "You want it slow?" he murmured, sliding one hand up her stomach. "Or rough?" "Trace..." "Say it." "Rough," she gasped. "God—yes." He grinned. "Good girl." He took control with the ease of a man who knew exactly what he was doing and exactly how she'd respond. Told her how good she tasted, how sweet she sounded, how fucking perfect she felt wrapped around him. Every stroke of his hips drove deeper, each thrust dragging sounds out of her she hadn't made in years—raw, honest, wrecked. His voice never stopped. "You feel that, Flip-Flops? That's mine now. Every inch of you. Mine." "Say it," he growled, voice ragged, hand tightening on her hip. She gasped, fingers clawing at his shoulders. "Yours." "Say it louder." "Yours, Trace." He grinned, savage and satisfied. "Damn right."

They didn't stop after once. Or twice. They moved from the couch to the wall to the floor, the night stretching out in waves of sweat and tangled sheets, whispered names and open-mouthed kisses. When he bent her over the kitchen table and pulled her back against him with a guttural sound in his throat, she didn't beg him to stop—she begged for more. He gave it to her. By the time they collapsed into bed, Mae's body was trembling, her voice gone, her pulse still pounding. Trace kissed her shoulder, then her spine, curling around her like armor. "Still mad I didn't deny it?" Mae looked up, smiling, hair wild and skin kissed with heat. "Ask me again after breakfast." He grinned. "Challenge accepted."

Chapter 20

Cockblocked by Carbs

Mae woke to the smell of coffee and the low hum of Trace's voice. At first, she thought it was a dream—too perfect, too cozy. But the murmur of conversation and the faint scent of cinnamon meant otherwise. Her body ached in all the right places, a slow, satisfying soreness that reminded her just how thoroughly she'd been worshipped the night before. She stretched beneath the sheets, dragging her fingers across the fabric where Trace had slept. Still warm. Slipping out of bed, she tugged on one of his shirts—worn soft, a little too big, smelling like him—and padded into the kitchen, her hair a wreck and her heart strangely steady.

Trace stood barefoot by the counter, phone cradled to his ear and a pan of cinnamon rolls in the oven. He was still shirtless, tattoos vivid in the morning light, low-slung sweatpants hanging in that unfair way. When he saw her, his gaze softened instantly. "Yeah, I'll be there by noon," he said into the phone, eyes locked on Mae. "Nah, just grabbing some breakfast first. Yeah. Uh-huh. Later." He ended the call and set the phone on the counter. "Morning, Flip-Flops." She leaned against the doorway, arms crossed, pretending like her knees weren't made of Jell-O. "You baked?" He shrugged, grinning. "The can exploded in my hand. Very dramatic. You missed it." Mae walked over, toes curling on the tile, and stood on tiptoe to steal a sip from his mug. "Smells good." "You do too," he said, voice dipping just enough to make her feel it in her stomach. She smirked, taking another sip. "Flatter me again and I'll let you feed me one." "Oh, sweetheart," he said, stepping closer, hand sliding around her waist, "if I start feeding you, I'm not stopping at cinnamon rolls."

Mae laughed, then caught her breath as his hand slid lower, cupping her bare thigh beneath the hem of the shirt. She pressed a kiss to his jaw, then another beneath his ear. "Don't start something you don't have time to finish," she whispered. "Oh, I have time. I'll be late to my own funeral for this." She squealed as he picked her up and set her on the counter, his body already slotting between her thighs. The oven dinged behind him. "Breakfast can wait," he muttered. "I love a man with priorities," Mae said, her fingers curling into his hair. They kissed slow and deep, the kind of kiss that made the world tilt just a little. When they finally pulled apart, breathless and flushed, Trace rested his forehead against hers. "You're trouble." "You invited me into your kitchen. That's on you."

They shared sticky bites of cinnamon rolls, his fingers feeding her pieces before licking the icing from her lips. She fed him back, smearing a swipe of frosting across his collarbone just so she could clean it with her tongue. At one point, she leaned in for a kiss, only to have him dodge and grab another bite instead. "Did you just cockblock me with carbs?" she gasped. Trace grinned, licking icing from his thumb. "Sweetheart, if I'm getting cockblocked, it's gonna be something worth it. These rolls? Worth it." Laughter echoed through the apartment like music—easy and unfiltered. They sat at the kitchen table with legs tangled and plates mostly empty, talking about everything and nothing. He told her stories from the track, she filled in details about Beckett's last science fair. Somewhere between a joke about motocross groupies and a heated debate over the best cereal, he reached across the table and touched her wrist. "This feels real." Mae didn't look away. "It is."

Eventually, Trace stood, gathering his things with slow reluctance. He kissed her again in the doorway, hands fisting the back of her shirt like he hated the idea of leaving. "I'll see you tonight?" She nodded, unable to do anything else. Trace left with cinnamon icing on his collar and her lip gloss on his cheek. Mae watched him go with her coffee in hand and a ridiculous smile she couldn't shake. This wasn't just fun anymore. This was something. And she wasn't afraid of it. Not today.

Chapter 21

Full Throttle & Front Row

By the time Mae arrived at the track that evening, the sun had started its slow descent, spilling gold across the world like a secret worth whispering. Everything shimmered—chrome bikes, lifted dust, the buzz of fans perched along fences with cups in hand and grit on their faces. The air smelled like engine oil, heat, and popcorn, and beneath it all, the hum of anticipation rose like a second heartbeat. She walked past rows of trailers and merch tents, VIP badge swinging against her chest, boots kicking up little clouds of dirt. The crowd was loud but happy, that special kind of electric that only came from people waiting to watch something reckless unfold. Trace wasn't on the track yet. He was tucked under a branded canopy near the pit area, his team in full prep mode. Someone was adjusting his bike's front forks. Another guy in the aviators was tossing back a water bottle while jotting down tire pressure notes. Trace stood in the center of it all—confident, gear halfway zipped, laughing at something one of his teammates had said. And then he saw her. Whatever was funny faded from his expression like mist in the heat. His mouth tugged into a slow smile—lazy, lethal, and aimed entirely at her.

Trace broke from the group like the earth had tilted in her direction, walking with that same unhurried confidence that never failed to steal her breath. It wasn't cocky. It wasn't even intentional. It was just *him.* Shoulders relaxed, strides long, sweat-darkened collar clinging to the base of his throat, a smear of grease on his forearm. He looked like trouble and victory wrapped in one perfect package. "Look what the sunset dragged in," he said when he reached her, voice low and lined with amusement. "My favorite distraction." Mae tilted her head. "Am I supposed to apologize for that?" His eyes dropped to her mouth, then lower, lingering just long enough to send heat pooling low in her stomach. "Not even a little. But I might need you to make up for it later." She smirked. "Don't threaten me with a good time, Jagger." He stepped in just enough that her breath hitched. Not touching. Not yet. But the air between them went tight, hot, charged. Like lightning coiling before the strike. She could feel the smirk on his lips before she saw it. "You wore red," he said. "You like red." "I like you in anything. Especially out of it." She snorted. "Charming." "That's what the tabloids said this morning." Mae rolled her eyes. "Oh, I saw. I especially liked the part where I was referred to as 'the anonymous firecracker in the paddock.' Very subtle." Trace leaned down, brushing his mouth against her ear, voice dipped low enough to make her toes curl. "I don't want you to be anonymous. I want you front and center." Before she could respond with something smart—and maybe a little desperate—the loudspeaker crackled overhead. "First call: Pro Heat One. Riders to staging." Trace exhaled, his forehead pressing to hers for a heartbeat. "Guess that's me." "Guess so," she murmured, barely able to hide the twist in her stomach. He pulled back, eyes scanning her face like he was committing it to memory. "Stay close. I want you to see what I look like when I'm all adrenaline and ego." Mae raised a brow. "So… same as usual?" His grin split wide. "Watch it.

That mouth's gonna get you in trouble." She grinned back. "That's the goal."

Then he was gone—walking toward the staging area with that same effortless energy, team flanking him, the low rumble of his bike starting like a growl beneath the hum of the crowd. And Mae? She stayed right where he told her to. Close. Because something about that look he gave her—like she was the only thing in the world that mattered—made her want to see *everything.* Especially the parts of him he only showed when he was flying down a track, full throttle and fearless.

The race was brutal—tight corners, high jumps, riders so close they could taste each other's tire spray. Mae stood near the edge of the VIP box, eyes locked on Trace's number. He took the holeshot off the gate, leading early, but two other riders were right on his tail. Beckett would've lost his mind narrating this. Lap after lap, Trace rode like he had something to prove. Controlled chaos. One hand on the throttle, the other on her heart, it felt like. Mae watched him fly off a berm, land clean, then angle around the whoops without losing a beat. Then came the final lap. Trace was neck-and-neck with a rider in blue, the crowd on their feet. She couldn't breathe. And then—Trace took the inside corner like a man possessed, shot through the final straight, and crossed the line first. Victory exploded around them. Fireworks, airhorns, the announcer shouting his name over the roar. Mae didn't even realize she was crying until she tasted salt.

The post-race celebration was chaotic. Trace was lifted onto the podium, champagne sprayed like victory confetti, and cameras flashed. He held up the trophy, wiped sweat from his brow, and searched the crowd until he found her. Their eyes locked. That wink again—slow, deliberate, like he'd planned it all along. She was already waiting by the trailer when he finally peeled away from the crowd. Helmet under one arm, sweat-slick hair curling at his temples, dirt streaked down his jaw. He looked like sin in technicolor. "Still my favorite distraction?" she asked. He didn't answer. Just grabbed her hand and pulled her into the trailer.

The door slammed. The silence hit. Then Trace. "You wore that dress on purpose, didn't you?" he asked, voice low and dangerous. "Maybe." "You know what that means?" She barely had time to shake her head before he was on her. Mouth hungry, hands everywhere, like he needed to taste her to survive. She hit the wall with a thud, legs wrapping around him instinctively. "You drive me insane," he growled against her throat. "You walk into my world, mess with my head, and then act like you don't know what you're doing." She gasped as his hand slid under her dress. "I know exactly what I'm doing." He smirked. "Good. Because I'm about to remind you why you never forget a Jagger ride." Clothes hit the floor. The tiny couch groaned. Her moan echoed off the walls. "God, Trace—" "Say my name like that again, and I'll make you forget yours." She clawed at his shoulders, back arching. "Someone might hear." He didn't slow down. "Then let 'em. Let them know exactly who's got you this wrecked."

Every kiss, every thrust, every curse against her skin was heat and possession and something terrifyingly close to love. And when he finally pushed her over the edge, her cry was muffled against his chest. They collapsed in a tangle of limbs and panting breaths, the air thick with sweat and satisfaction. His hand smoothed up her side, lips brushing her temple. "You good?" She nodded, breathless. "Better than good." "Good. Because we're not done yet. Not even close." And with the crowd still cheering outside, Trace showed her exactly what victory tasted like—again and again.

Chapter 22

Cool Down Laps & Close Calls

The morning after the race, the air still buzzed with the high of the win. Mae stirred in the hotel bed, tangled in warm sheets and remnants of the night before. Trace was already up, barefoot by the window, phone to his ear, talking to someone about a press shoot later that day. He wore nothing but a pair of athletic shorts, and his back—bare, broad, tattooed—looked even more dangerous in the early light. She sat up slowly, the sheet falling to her waist. "You planning to start without me?" Trace turned, a smirk already forming. "Wouldn't dare. Gimme five minutes." He wrapped up the call, tossed the phone onto the chair, and walked over with the kind of swagger that should be illegal before 9 a.m. "You hungry? Room service or another round of cardio?" Mae chuckled, leaning back on her elbows. "Depends—does the hotel serve post-coital waffles?" He leaned down, kissed the corner of her mouth. "Only if you let me watch you eat them."

They ordered breakfast—pancakes, bacon, and enough coffee to caffeinate a biker rally—and ate on the balcony, overlooking the parking lot and the dusty edges of the makeshift track. Fans were already starting to gather around the gates again, hoping for autographs or selfies. Mae took a long sip of her coffee. "You know they're going to keep coming now, right? After that win? After last night?" Trace stretched his arms overhead, the muscles in his stomach flexing. "Let 'em. I've got nothing to hide." She raised a brow. "You sure about that?" He glanced at her. "You nervous?" Mae didn't answer right away. She watched a group of teens dart across the lot in matching Trace Jagger t-shirts. The fan energy was palpable. She was in it now—his world, his spotlight. "Not nervous," she finally said. "Just... aware." Trace leaned across the tiny table, resting his chin in his hand. "Of what?" She met his gaze. "That this feels too good to be easy." He didn't flinch. Didn't smirk. Just nodded once, slow and serious. "Maybe it's not supposed to be easy. Maybe it's just supposed to be worth it." She reached for his hand. Their fingers locked like puzzle pieces.

Later that afternoon, Trace had a sponsor meeting and a brief on-camera segment, so Mae wandered around the fan zone, sunglasses on and hoodie pulled low over her forehead. She wasn't trying to be mysterious—just needed a little space to think. A girl at the merch booth pointed at her quietly, whispering to her friend. Mae smiled politely and kept walking. She wasn't famous. Not really. But she was clearly someone. And someone meant eyes. She ducked into one of the quieter food tents, grabbed an overpriced lemonade, and found a shady spot behind the trailers. Her phone buzzed.

Tori: Everything okay?

Mae: Yeah. Just breathing.

Tori: Good. Breathe in the hot racer sex. Breathe out the drama.

Mae: You are wildly unhelpful.

Tori: You're welcome.

Mae smiled, pocketed her phone, and let herself enjoy the quiet for a few minutes.

When Trace found her again, he was flushed from the cameras, hat low over his eyes, and grinning like a man who had secrets. "Wanna sneak out for the rest of the afternoon?" She stood. "Thought you'd never ask." They took the Bronco down a winding service road that led to a small lake. It wasn't exactly a hidden getaway, but it was quiet enough, surrounded by trees and just remote enough that no one followed them. Trace parked under the shade of a sprawling oak. "We've got about three hours before my next press call." Mae kicked off her shoes, sliding out of the passenger seat. "Better make 'em count."

They stretched out a blanket in the back of the Bronco, legs tangled, shoulders brushing. At first, they just talked—about random things. Childhood memories. First bikes. Worst injuries. "Broke my collarbone doing a wheelie at twelve," Trace said, popping a peanut into his mouth. "Tried to lie to my mom and say I tripped over the dog." Mae laughed. "And she believed that?" "She didn't. Grounded me for a month. I raced anyway." "Of course you did." He studied her then, eyes narrowing slightly like he was trying to memorize her all over again. "What about you? Worst decision you ever made?" She didn't hesitate. "Not kissing you that first night." Trace went still. Then leaned forward and kissed her like she had just rewritten his entire past. The blanket became a stage. Every kiss is deeper. Every whisper is louder. They moved together like they'd done it a hundred times, like this moment had been waiting for them all along. Mae moaned into his mouth, fingers fisting in his shirt. Trace bit her bottom lip, just enough to make her gasp. "Want you," he growled. "Now. Here." She nodded, already tugging at his belt. "Yes. Please." They didn't care about timing. Or the fact that anyone could stumble across them. The risk only made it hotter. He laid her back on the blanket, fingers running up her thighs, mouth trailing fire across her collarbone. "So goddamn beautiful," he muttered, pulling her panties down her legs. "You have no idea what you do to me." "Show me." And he did.

Every inch. Every sound. Every second burned into her. He took his time and lost it all at once—slow touches that turned to rough thrusts, her name rasped into the hollow of her throat. His voice was filth and worship, dominance laced with something tender. "You feel so fucking good, baby. Can't get enough. Gonna ruin you." Her hands gripped his shoulders, nails scraping as her breath caught. "Don't stop. Please—" "I won't. Not until you forget every name but mine." He drove into her again, and her cry cracked the quiet like thunder. And when he finally pushed her over the edge, her cry was muffled against his chest. She blinked up at him. "So... this is your idea of a cool down lap?" He laughed, breathless. "You have no idea." They lay there for a while longer, catching their breath, tangled and quiet. No jokes. No racing thoughts. Just the hum of victory outside the trailer—and the thrill of something even better inside it.

Chapter 23

Promises & Pasta

They ate standing up in the kitchen, barefoot on the cool tile, plates balanced in one hand while the other passed the wine bottle back and forth like a secret they weren't ready to say out loud. The meal was simple—pasta, warm bread, something Trace had thrown together with the kind of chaotic confidence he used for everything else. Mae didn't even know if it was good. She wasn't paying attention to the food. Every once in a while, his fingers would brush her hip when he reached for the bottle, casual and slow—just enough to make her breath catch. And sometimes she'd lean into his arm without meaning to, like her body was learning a rhythm she hadn't agreed to yet.

The music playing from the speaker was low and jazzy, some playlist Trace had claimed was "mood-enhancing, not seductive"—which only made her laugh and blush harder every time the saxophone kicked in. Their conversation was light. Teasing. Safe. Favorite movies, worst tattoos, ridiculous fan encounters. But beneath the words, something unspoken pulsed in the silence between beats. When she laughed too hard at one of his stories, she didn't notice how close they were until she turned and found her face inches from his chest. She didn't step back. Her breath hitched, caught between the wine and the weight of everything unsaid. Trace's eyes dropped to her mouth, lingered there, then rose again with a heat that curled through her stomach.

They didn't talk about what it meant. Not yet. Because whatever *this* was—it was still unfolding. Still unwrapping itself in glances and soft laughter and the way his eyes lingered too long on her mouth when she smiled. She took the bottle from his hand, drank straight from it, then held it out to him with a smirk. "This counts as a date, right?" Trace leaned down, took the bottle, and sipped without looking away from her. "It counts as a promise." Mae felt that in her spine. They finished the wine, but neither of them moved. Not right away. Because the space between them had become something electric. Something waiting. And neither of them was ready to turn off the lights just yet. Trace set the bottle down with a quiet thud, then reached for her waist. "I've been trying to be good," he murmured against her temple. "Trying not to rush this." Her voice came out softer than she meant. "Don't."

The kiss started slowly. Measured. A question and an answer all at once. But the moment her hands slid under his shirt and traced the lines of his stomach, it changed. Trace lifted her easily onto the counter, stepped between her thighs, and kissed her like he needed to remind her of every reason he'd waited. "Take this off," he said, tugging gently at the hem of her tank top. She obeyed, pulling it over her head. He stepped back just long enough to let his eyes drag over every inch of her, slow and reverent. "You're dangerous like this," he said, voice low. "Standing in my kitchen. Looking like a fantasy I didn't know I had." She reached for him, pulled his mouth back to hers. "Then do something about it." Trace groaned against her lips, peeled off his shirt, and pressed her flat against the counter. His hands slid up her thighs, fingers curling into the softness of her hips. "I'm going to ruin you for anyone else," he said, biting gently at the spot just beneath her ear. Mae gasped, nails digging into his back. "Too late."

The rest of her clothes disappeared piece by piece. His mouth followed the trail his hands made—down her chest, across her stomach, until she was shaking and begging and breathless. And when he finally pressed into her, her cry echoed off the kitchen walls. They didn't make it to the bedroom. Didn't care. The counter was unforgiving, but his touch wasn't. He kissed her through every thrust, every moan, every tremble. He told her how good she felt, how long he'd wanted this, how she made him lose control in the best way. His voice was rough against her skin, a constant low stream of praise and possession. Her back arched, fingers gripping his shoulders, her legs wrapped tight around his waist as he drove into her with a rhythm that said he knew exactly what she needed.

Every kiss, every thrust, every curse against her skin was heat and possession and something terrifyingly close to love. They collapsed in a tangle of limbs and panting breaths, the air thick with sweat and satisfaction. Trace held her, forehead pressed to hers, their breaths syncing, the heat between them still simmering. Afterward, he wrapped her in a dish towel like it was a blanket and kissed her forehead. "Next time," he said, still breathless, "we're doing that with actual bedding." Mae laughed against his chest. "You mean there's going to be a next time?" He smirked, kissed her again, and whispered against her mouth, "Try and stop me."

Chapter 24

First Place, Fast Hands

The next morning, sunlight filtered through the slats of the blinds, cutting soft gold lines across Trace's bare back. Mae stirred slowly, her legs tangled in a too-thin sheet, her body still humming from the night before. Every inch of her ached in the best way—like she'd run a marathon of pleasure and slept in a bed made of satisfaction and sin. Trace was already awake, propped on one elbow beside her, watching her like she was some kind of miracle. "You stare like you're trying to memorize me," she mumbled, blinking at the light. "That's exactly what I'm doing," he said. "Don't move. I like this view." She stretched lazily, the sheet falling away to reveal bare skin. Trace groaned. "That's just mean," he muttered, dragging his fingers slowly over her hip. "I have a morning meeting in an hour. Now I'm going to walk in looking like I've been hit by a sex truck." Mae laughed and reached up to brush a hand through his messy hair. "You'll survive." He leaned down, kissed her slowly, then rolled out of bed with a stretch. "Shower with me?" She arched an eyebrow. "Is that your idea of multitasking?" "I'm just trying to conserve water. I'm eco-conscious." "Of course you are." Still, she followed him into the bathroom, the door clicking shut behind them. They made it downstairs an hour later, dressed, fed, and barely on time. Trace grabbed his duffel while Mae leaned in the doorway, watching him tug on his boots. "You nervous?" she asked. He paused, then gave a short shrug. "Not about the race." Mae frowned. "What, then?" He stood, walked over, and tucked a strand of hair behind her ear. "About how much I want this to last." She opened her mouth, but the words got stuck. So she kissed him instead. It wasn't a goodbye. It wasn't even a see-you-later. It was a promise, quietly made in the space between them.

At the track, the energy was electric—almost oppressive, like the air itself vibrated with piston thunder and crowd noise. Fans pressed shoulder-to-shoulder along the fences, jerseys flapping in a dry breeze that smelled like rubber, dust, and sizzling food-truck grease. EDM bass rolled through the grandstands, making bleachers rattle and hearts thump in sync. Trace had his game face on: goggles resting on the visor of his helmet, gloves tucked under an arm, head bent with his crew chief over a clipboard of lap strategies. Even from fifty feet away Mae could read the tension in his shoulders—coiled, ready to strike. A sponsor shot photos; Trace barely blinked, eyes already on the starting gate. Mae wedged herself against the pit fence, knuckles white around the chain-link. Her phone buzzed.

Tori: *You better scream louder than the engines today.*

Mae: *I plan to.*

The gate dropped with a metallic snap. Trace rocketed forward, rear tire spitting roost that peppered the first row. He carved inside on Turn 1, handlebars brushing berm, suspension compressing so hard Mae felt it in her knees. Mid-pack chaos erupted—two bikes tangled, another rider high-sided—but Trace danced through it like gravity was optional. Lap after lap he built a lead, scrubbing jumps low, drive chain screaming a war song. Announcers lost their minds: "Jagger is *sending* it—look at that corner speed!" Mae's throat went raw from shouting, her pulse trying to outrun his rev limiter. Final lap. Blue-flagged lappers scattered as Trace charged, chest over bars, elbows out. He hit the last rhythm section almost sideways, landed clean, and pinned it down the straight. Checkered flag. First place by three seconds. Mae's eyes burned; she didn't realize she was crying until dust stuck to her tears. Trace coasted toward the podium, popped the visor, and, before the champagne or interviews, found her in the crush of people. He tapped his chestplate, pointed straight at her, and mouthed, *"That's for you, Flip-Flops."*

The trailer door slammed; the roar outside fell away. Trace dropped the trophy on a bench cushion, yanked off his jersey, sweat steaming in the AC blast. Mae barely got "You ride like that just to get la—" out before he pinned her to the aluminum wall, lips devouring the rest. She tasted adrenaline, Gatorade, and dust. Helmet hair stuck up in wild spikes; she loved it. "Only when it works," he growled, hitching her thigh over his hip. Body armor clattered to the floor. Gloves, chest protector, her tank top—everything peeled away in frantic layers until skin met overheated skin.

They didn't need a bed. The narrow counter bit into Mae's lower back; she didn't care. Trace's mouth branded a path down her throat, teeth scraping, tongue soothing. He pressed inside her in one fierce glide that punched a gasp from her lungs. "Still shaking from the gate drop," he panted against her ear. "Feel that? That's *you*." Mae answered with a moan that sounded suspiciously like his name. Her nails raked sweaty shoulders as he set a punishing rhythm—fast, deep, desperate. Every thrust rattled cabinet doors; somewhere a socket wrench hit the floor. Pleasure coiled, tight and hot. He slipped a hand between them, thumb circling until her vision sparked white. She shattered, bite muffled against the curve of his neck. Trace followed moments later, groan ripped from his chest like the last roar of the race. They slumped together, breaths jagged, foreheads pressed. Outside, the crowd still cheered—but in the small metal box of the trailer, there was only the thrum of cooling engines and the slower, steadier cadence of two hearts finally catching up. Mae brushed damp hair from his eyes. "You win trophies for that too?" Trace chuckled, nipped her bottom lip. "Only need one prize." He'd already found what he wanted. Her.

Chapter 25

Couchlight Confessions

The following day dawned quieter, the buzz of race day replaced by a more intimate kind of adrenaline. Trace and Mae had checked out of the hotel just after breakfast—waffles from the fabled pancake robot, coffee strong enough to raise the dead, and enough side glances across the booth to fuel a dozen new rumors. Trace drove with one hand on the wheel, the other alternating between resting on Mae's thigh and fiddling with the radio. They didn't talk much—not because there was nothing to say, but because some silences were more honest than words. "You know," Trace said at one point, eyes still on the road, "I could get used to this." Mae turned to look at him. "Driving hungover with your gear still sweaty in the back?" "No," he smirked. "You. In my passenger seat. Looking at me like you know how I like my eggs and how I come undone." Mae flushed, but didn't look away. "You do fall apart in very specific ways." He chuckled. "And you take me apart like it's your favorite hobby."

They stopped halfway to stretch their legs and refill coffee. Mae leaned against the truck while Trace talked to a fan who recognized him even in sunglasses. She watched the way he engaged—charming, patient, not the aloof adrenaline junkie people painted him as. Back on the road, the city began to rise in the distance—familiar, a little less magical than the weekend haze they were coming down from. "Tell me something I don't know about you," Mae said suddenly, breaking the lull. Trace didn't hesitate. "I hate bananas. Like, full-body cringe hate." She laughed. "Seriously? That's your deep confession?" He grinned. "I also cried the first time I watched *The Iron Giant*. Don't tell anyone." Mae rested her feet on the dash, turning slightly toward him. "Your secret's safe with me. But only if you tell me what your go-to karaoke song is." Trace groaned. "God. 'Living on a Prayer.' Don't ask why. It's spiritual." She nearly snorted her coffee. "That actually makes so much sense." They kept going, questions tumbling naturally between them like a well-worn game of catch. She told him she used to want to be a marine biologist until she realized how much science was involved. He admitted he once kissed a girl just to make an ex jealous—spoiler: it backfired. They debated the best pizza topping combinations, whether ghosts were real, and who would survive longer in a zombie apocalypse. (Trace swore it was her. Mae didn't argue.)

By the time they pulled into her driveway, it felt like hours had passed in minutes. The house was still, Tori and Beckett still gone, leaving them in a rare pocket of uninterrupted time. Trace killed the engine. "Mind if I hang out a little?" "Only if you're willing to risk a lukewarm cup of last-week's tea." He leaned over and kissed her. "Risk accepted." Inside, Mae dropped her bag by the door and headed toward the kitchen. Trace followed, slower, eyes scanning her home with casual curiosity. "You're not what I expected," he said softly. She looked over her shoulder. "What did you expect?" He shrugged. "More walls. More defenses. Fewer glitter signs in the hallway." "You caught me in a vulnerable moment. I'm usually way more intimidating." "Terrifying," he teased. She turned around, arms crossed. "You're not so tough either." He stepped forward, crowding into her space. "I think you like that about me." "I plead the fifth." The air between them thickened with unsaid things, but instead of giving into it, they curled up on the couch, legs tangled, the late afternoon sun making the room feel wrapped in gold. They talked about everything—favorite movies, weird dreams, irrational fears. Trace admitted he once bought a vintage motorcycle just because it reminded him of a comic book he read as a kid. Mae confessed she secretly loved bad reality shows and cried during cooking competitions. They laughed until their stomachs hurt, paused only to sip from mismatched mugs, and occasionally kissed like it was punctuation. "If you could be anywhere in the world right now, where would you be?" she asked. He looked at her. "Here." She rolled her eyes. "That's such a line." "It's not a line if it's true." Mae let that hang in the air for a beat too long before nudging him with her foot. "You're such a sap." "You bring it out of me." Their laughter faded into soft touches, fingers brushing over arms, shoulders, hands. And for once, it wasn't about what came next. It was about now.

The sun sank lower. The room darkened. But neither moved to turn on the lights. It was enough to just be—two people on a couch, wrapped in each other and conversation. Trace pulled the blanket over their legs and laid his head back against the couch. "You ever think about what it would've been like if we'd met years ago?" Mae tilted her head. "You mean like, younger and dumber?" He smiled. "Yeah. Think I would've fallen for you faster." She traced lazy circles on his chest. "I would've run. I wasn't ready then." "You're ready now?" She met his eyes. "I think... I want to be." Trace leaned in, kissed her gently. It wasn't about heat or need. It was about comfort. Reassurance. A quiet kind of yes.

Later, when the room was nothing but shadows and soft breathing, they stayed exactly where they were—no rush, no pretending. Just them. And for the first time, Mae didn't want to overthink it. Because this wasn't some fleeting weekend fantasy. This was something deeper. This was her and Trace Jagger. Just being them.

Chapter 26

Dream Dirty, Stay Soft

Mae didn't expect the week to pass quietly. Not after the weekend they'd just had. But somehow, everything felt more settled than chaotic—like the dust had finally started to land after the last few months of upheaval. Beckett returned home late Sunday evening, full of stories about Tori's attempt at microwave pancakes, a Nerf gun war that nearly broke a lamp, and how he was now the reigning champion of Mario Kart in their friend group. Mae hugged him tighter than she meant to. He didn't complain. Trace didn't stay that night, but he texted her goodnight.

Trace: Dream of me. But like… the PG version.

Mae: Sorry, already dreaming of you making pancakes shirtless.

Trace: That's at least PG-13.

Mae: So is your smile.

They kept texting late into the night, teasing and soft and occasionally slipping into something darker. Something needier.

Trace: You keep texting like that, I'm not gonna sleep.

Mae: Who said I wanted you to?

Trace: Oh, you want me restless? Desperate? Lying in bed thinking about the way you taste?

Mae: Maybe.

Trace: Then I hope you know I'm hard as hell right now.

Mae: I'd ask for proof, but I don't think either of us would sleep then.

Trace: You say that like it's a bad thing.

Mae: Fine. Tell me what you'd do if you were here.

Trace: Pull you into my lap. Kiss you until you forget what you were thinking. Then slide your panties to the side and taste you until you're shaking.

Mae: Jesus.

Trace: Nope. Just me. On my knees. Addicted.

Mae: Keep going.

Trace: I'd take my time. One hand in your hair. The other on your hip. Tongue working you open until you're whimpering my name. And then I'd fuck you slow. Deep. Like I want it to echo in your bones.

Mae: I'm never sleeping again.

Trace: Good. I want you tired tomorrow. Needy. Thinking about what we could've done if I was there.

Mae: I already am.

Trace: One day, baby. I'll whisper it all in your ear instead of through a screen. I'll ruin you properly.

Mae: Promise?

Trace: Cross my goddamn heart.

They didn't stop. Not for a while. The conversation shifted between soft and dirty, want and warmth. He'd flirt, then turn reverent. He'd tease, then say something so sincere it made her chest ache.

Trace: You're the only person who makes me laugh and lose my mind in the same breath.

Mae: You're dangerous.

Trace: Only for you.

Mae: I like that.

Eventually, her replies slowed. One dot. Then another. Then nothing.

Trace sent one more message.

Trace: Sleep tight, Flip-Flops. Dream dirty. I'll see you soon.

    She didn't even remember when she finally fell asleep—only that her last thought was of him, his voice in her head, and the way he made her feel like the only girl in the world worth texting at 1:47 a.m. By Tuesday, she found herself reorganizing her cabinets. Not because they needed it, but because she needed the distraction. She didn't hear the door until it opened.

    Trace walked in like he'd always belonged there—carrying a bag of groceries and a crooked grin. "I brought bribes." Mae blinked. "What kind of bribes?" "Pasta, garlic bread, and the promise of backrubs if I burn everything." "You cook now?" she asked, crossing her arms. "I attempt," he said, brushing past her and heading into the kitchen. "You coming or just going to stare at my ass all day?" Mae followed, not bothering to answer. They cooked side by side. Or, rather, Mae did most of the supervising while Trace tried not to chop his own fingers off. Somehow, they made it work. The sauce simmered. Garlic filled the room. Trace insisted on feeding her a bite straight from the spoon—she let him, despite the mess.

    Dinner was loud and unpolished, laughter woven between every mouthful. They spilled sauce, knocked over a glass of wine, and still ended up tangled together on the couch again. This time, though, the quiet didn't feel like a pause. It felt like permission. They didn't need music. Or candlelight. Or perfect timing. They had each other. Trace looked down at her, brushing a thumb along her cheekbone. "You know, I never thought I'd be the type to like this part." "What part?" "This," he said, gesturing vaguely between them. "The normal part. Dinner. Dishes. You're yelling at me for almost using dish soap in the pasta." Mae smirked. "You mean the domestic bliss part?" "Yeah. That." She let her hand rest over his heart. "I think you're better at it than you know." He bent down and kissed her—soft and slow and patient.

When it deepened, it wasn't frantic. It was careful. Thoughtful. His hands moved beneath her shirt with a reverence that made her heart ache. "I don't want fast tonight," he murmured. "I want to feel all of it." And he did. Every inch. Every sigh. Every piece of her that had been waiting for something real. After, they lay tangled in sheets, the scent of garlic still faint in the air and the warmth of his skin grounding her. They talked again—this time about futures. Not in concrete ways. Not about moving in or rings or timelines. But about wants. Dreams. Fears.

Trace told her about the moment he realized racing was more than a sport to him. How he'd broken his wrist at sixteen and thought it was over. How he cried harder than he ever had when he got back on the bike a year later and realized it still made his heart race. Mae told him about her art degree she never used. The paintings still boxed up in her attic. The one she'd almost sold once but pulled last minute because it felt like letting go of something she wasn't ready to. "You should show me sometime," he said. "Only if you promise not to laugh." "I won't," he said. "Unless you painted me with abs I clearly don't have." She laughed, and he kissed the sound right off her lips. When they finally fell asleep, it was with his arm around her waist and her fingers tucked against his chest. And for the first time in a long time, Mae didn't feel like she had to brace for the fall. She just let herself float.

Chapter 27

Waffles & Whispers

By Thursday, Mae was buzzing. Not in the caffeine-overload way. Not even in the lingering-afterglow kind of way. This was different. It was anticipation, warm and tight in her chest. Like something big was coming. Like the good kind of storm. Trace had a race that weekend—one of the bigger ones. Out-of-town, high-stakes, broadcast-on-TV kind of event. Beckett was going to Tori's again, this time with explicit permission to eat as many snacks as humanly possible and a warning not to talk Trace's ear off via FaceTime. Mae was packed by Thursday night. One bag. Three outfits. Too many hopes she wasn't ready to unpack. Friday morning, Trace picked her up in the Bronco, this time freshly washed and stocked with two iced coffees and a playlist that felt suspiciously curated. "Tell me you didn't make a road trip playlist," she teased. "I make no apologies for my taste in music," he said, sliding on sunglasses. "Also, if 'Gimme Shelter' comes on and you don't sing harmony, we're breaking up." "Oh, we're dating now?" He grinned. "Don't make me put a label on it. I'm fragile."

The drive was hours of back-and-forth banter, snacks, shared glances, and near-constant hand-holding across the console. Trace drove like he raced—aggressively smooth, always in control, always just fast enough to keep her breath caught halfway in her chest. They got to the hotel by early evening. It was nicer than Mae expected. Clean, warm, with real sheets and a view of the track in the distance. "Not bad," she said, kicking off her shoes. "I save the roach motels for solo trips," he said, tossing her a water bottle. "You get a good thread count." She arched her brow. "Because you like me or because I'm high-maintenance?" "Both." They didn't leave the hotel that night.

Instead, they curled into each other on the too-firm mattress, limbs tangled and laughter muted by soft sheets and soft confessions. They talked about everything—from the worst race injuries to best childhood memories. Trace told her about his sister who lived in Oregon and called once a month to make sure he wasn't dead. Mae told him about her dad's old record player and the way she used to fall asleep to Fleetwood Mac. And sometime around midnight, when her head was tucked under his chin and his thumb was lazily tracing patterns on her hip, he said it. Not loud. Not like a grand gesture. But soft. Honest. "I think I'm falling in love with you." Mae didn't move. Didn't breathe. But her heart answered before her lips did. "I think I already did." They didn't sleep much after that. Not because of nerves. But because kissing someone who just made you feel like the center of their universe is addictive. And because Trace Jagger had a way of turning whispers into worship.

The next morning, they woke late—sunlight slipping between the cheap hotel curtains in lazy stripes, casting everything in a warm, amber haze. The air still smelled faintly of skin and sleep and something softer neither of them dared name. Mae stretched under the sheets, groaning as she blinked at the clock. 9:12 a.m. Definitely late. Her legs tangled with

Trace's, his arm heavy across her stomach. She didn't want to move. Didn't want to do anything except soak in the feel of him beside her. But her stomach had other ideas. "I'm starving," she murmured, turning toward him. Trace didn't open his eyes. "There's a menu somewhere. Call room service. Order everything. Especially the waffles." Mae grinned. "You're very demanding for someone who nearly pulled a muscle last night." He cracked one eye open, smirking. "You wore my shirt. That makes you responsible for breakfast." "Is that how it works?" "House rules." She rolled out of bed and padded across the room, his oversized t-shirt barely covering her thighs. She picked up the room service menu, scanned it, and picked up the phone. He watched her from the bed, completely unbothered, hair a wreck and face half-buried in a pillow.

When the knock finally came, Mae opened the door just enough to accept the tray, and Trace whistled when she turned back around. "Definitely illegal how good you look right now," he said. Mae climbed back into bed beside him and handed him a cup of coffee. "Hydrate, racer boy." They ate sitting cross-legged on the bed, passing the coffee back and forth, stealing bites of waffle and bacon from each other's plates. "You're such a menace," Mae said as Trace attempted to balance syrup on his fork and flick it toward her. "Just keeping the energy up. You don't want me going into this race low on chaos." She tossed a strawberry at him, hitting him square in the chest. They laughed. They kissed. And somewhere between the orange juice and the stolen kisses, something settled in Mae. A knowing. A calm that didn't feel like settling—it felt like arriving.

Trace pulled on his gear slowly, deliberately. His race-day ritual, she'd come to understand. Focus in layers. Socks, then pants, then boots. Jersey last. Sunglasses perched on his head. "You gonna be okay without me for a few hours?" he asked, looping a lanyard with her VIP pass around her neck. Mae smirked. "Try to win. I'll see if I can find the pancake robot again." He grinned, leaned in, and kissed her like he meant it—like she was more than a good luck charm, more than a one-weekend flame. Like she was already a winner. And she kissed him back like he was her reason for waking up smiling. "Go destroy them," she whispered. Trace's eyes lingered on hers. "Only for you." Then he was gone—out the door and toward the track, leaving behind the faint scent of aftershave and adrenaline. Mae sat back on the bed, her fingers grazing the collar of his shirt still clinging to her shoulders. Whatever today brought, she already knew what she was rooting for. Him.

Chapter 28

Win Me. Wreck Me.

The stands were already half-full by the time Mae made it to the track. The roar of engines, the scent of oil and earth, the buzz of conversation—it all wrapped around her like a living pulse. Trace's name was already being thrown around by fans in matching shirts and kids with homemade signs. She couldn't help but smile. She found her spot in the VIP section, lanyard flashing, heart already racing. Trace hadn't messaged her yet, but she knew he was in the zone. Race days were different—he turned focused, quiet, electric. And when he finally appeared near the pit tent, gear zipped up, helmet tucked under one arm, her stomach flipped. Blue and white this time. His walk was all purpose and ease, the kind of confidence you couldn't fake. The kind that came from knowing exactly who the hell you were. He looked up, found her instantly, and smirked. She waved, pretending not to feel her knees turn to rubber.

Moments later, the announcer's voice boomed across the field, signaling the start of warmups. Trace gave her a final glance before slipping on his helmet and mounting his bike. The gate dropped. And the world erupted. Mae gripped the fence. The vibrations of the race moved through her feet and into her chest. Trace shot forward like he'd been launched, maneuvering with inhuman precision. Every jump, every turn, every lean into the corner had her holding her breath. He wasn't just racing—he was performing. By the halfway point, he'd taken the lead. But not by much. Number 12 was creeping up behind him, wheels clipping close, elbows flying at the curves. "Come on, Trace," she whispered, fingers white-knuckled around the railing. He dropped low into a turn, blocked the pass, then came out of it clean, engine screaming. Two laps to go. Her heart was a drumline. Her voice was raw from cheering. She couldn't even hear herself anymore. Last lap. Trace pulled ahead by half a second—then a full second. And then he crossed the finish line. First place. Mae's scream caught in her throat, joy and pride exploding through her like fireworks. Trace pulled off his helmet, sweaty hair falling into his face, and immediately turned toward her. He pointed. "That's for you, Flip-Flops," he mouthed. She didn't cry. Not really. Just a little moisture in her eyes. That's all.

Later, back at the trailer, the second the door shut, she was on him.Later, when the trailer door slammed behind them, Trace didn't waste a second. He spun her around, pressing her against the cabinets, breath still ragged from the win. "You know what you do to me?" he asked, voice rough in her ear. Mae barely had time to answer before his hands were under her shirt, dragging it over her head like it offended him. "I watched you cheering," he said, lips trailing fire along her collarbone. "Screaming my name like it already belonged to you." She gasped as he lifted her onto the counter. "It does." "Damn right it does." He kissed her then—fierce and focused, like he was chasing the high all over again. His hands gripped her thighs, pulling her closer until she couldn't tell where she ended and he began. "You win a lot," she whispered, breathless.

"Only the things that matter." Her head fell back, mouth parting on a moan as his tongue traced a path down her stomach. "Trace—" "No helmets. No cameras. Just me making you lose your mind." "I really do." He carried her across the small space, set her on the counter, and kissed her like he planned to win her all over again. "I want you noisy," he said, voice rough with need. "No helmets. No cameras. Just me—making you forget your own name." Mae's pulse thundered in her ears. Trace dropped to his knees, tugging her shorts down in one smooth motion. His grip on her thighs was firm, anchoring her in place. When he dragged his mouth over her, slow and devastating, her head fell back against the cabinet. A moan spilled from her throat, sharp and aching. He licked, sucked, murmured her name like a prayer and a threat. She was already trembling, fingers tangled in his hair. "That's it," he murmured between licks. "Louder." She clawed at the counter, nails scraping laminate, thighs tightening around his shoulders as her body arched into him. "Trace—God—" He didn't stop. Didn't rush. Every movement was calculated chaos—building, unraveling, demanding. And when she came, it was with a choked cry, his name broken into pieces on her lips. She barely had time to catch her breath before he stood, flipped her around, and bent her over the counter.

His voice was a growl against her ear. "Not done." Her body answered before her mouth could—hips grinding back into him, need overriding everything. He pushed inside her in one hard, perfect thrust. Mae shattered again—louder, messier, no longer capable of pretending she didn't need this man like oxygen. Every thrust was deep and deliberate. Hands on her hips. Teeth grazing her shoulder. Dirty words against sweat-slick skin. "I love the way you take it," he whispered. "Like you were made for this." She whimpered his name, helpless against the rhythm he set—one she couldn't outrun, couldn't deny, wouldn't dare try.

And when they came together, bodies locked and pulsing with heat, it felt like more than sex. It felt like surrender. Like choosing each other in the most primal, undeniable way. They stayed like that for a moment—just breathing. Just existing. Then he kissed the back of her neck, soft and slow. A contrast to the chaos. She turned in his arms, wrapped her legs around his waist again, and buried her face in his chest. "I like post-win you," she murmured. He chuckled. "You earned it." "No," she whispered. "You did."

Chapter 29

Raceday Residue

The sun had already begun to dip by the time Trace and Mae finally emerged from the trailer, both looking just shy of wrecked in the best way. Mae's hair was tousled, lips still swollen from the kisses they couldn't stop stealing. Trace looked smug and sinfully satisfied, one hand low on her back as they made their way across the lot. Fans still hovered, packing up coolers and folding chairs. Some caught sight of them and waved. Trace nodded, and didn't let go of her. They found his team near the pit, already halfway through teardown. One of the mechanics tossed Trace a water bottle. "Solid ride today, boss. You were possessed." Trace grinned, uncapping it. "Had a good luck charm." Mae elbowed him gently, but the blush on her cheeks gave her away. They hung around for another hour—talking, laughing, reliving the best turns of the race. Mae found herself caught up in it, swept into the world of gears and adrenaline, of riders recounting near-misses like bedtime stories. By the time they headed back to the hotel, it was dark. The ride was quiet in that soft, golden way shared only by people who'd touched something perfect that day. The kind of quiet where you didn't need words. Where presence was enough.

Back in the room, Trace kicked his boots off and collapsed back onto the bed. Mae stood near the window, looking out over the parking lot, wrapped in one of his oversized t-shirts again. Her arms folded loosely across her chest, her body still humming. "You okay?" Trace asked, voice rough with fatigue and something gentler. "Yeah," she said without turning. "Just...taking it in." "Taking what in?" She smiled to herself. "Everything. The race. The way those fans looked at you. The way you looked at me." "Like I wanted to kiss you senseless in front of two thousand people?" "Exactly." He sat up. "Regret not letting me?" She turned finally, eyes dancing. "Regret not stopping you." That was all he needed. He stood, crossed the room in three strides, and kissed her like he'd been holding his breath since the race. Her fingers tangled in his shirt, pulling him closer. "We don't have to rush back tomorrow," he whispered between kisses. "No?" "Nah. We could sleep in. Order something we'll regret. Stay in this bed all day." She laughed against his lips. "You're gonna get me addicted to this life." "Good. Then I don't have to let you go."

The rest of the night unfolded slow and sweet—like whiskey poured neat and meant to linger. They talked between kisses, half-laughed through stolen bites of leftover food, curled up under scratchy hotel sheets like teenagers with a secret. He traced lazy lines along her shoulder, her thigh, the dip of her spine. She told him about the time she tried to make a gingerbread house with Beckett and ended up using hot glue. He confessed that he once got kicked out of a race for mooning a rival during warmups. They laughed so hard they cried. Then they cried, then kissed, then laughed again. When the food ran out and the TV played low in the background, Trace reached for her again—this time slower. Gentler. Like he was memorizing her in pieces. Fingertips to cheekbone. Lips to shoulder. "You're trouble," he whispered, voice hoarse with affection and something a little like reverence. "You like trouble." "I love this trouble." Later, when she finally fell asleep on his chest, legs tangled with his, breathing soft against his ribs, Trace didn't move. Didn't dare. Because there, in a dingy hotel off the interstate, wrapped in motel linens and moonlight—he knew he'd already fallen. Hard. Fast. And without brakes.

Chapter 30

Storm Warning

The press tent buzzed with pre-race energy. Cameras flashed. Boom mics hovered. Sponsors shook hands while riders ducked into pockets of shade, laughing too loud and stretching out stiff muscles. Trace Jagger lingered just off-center stage—sunglasses on, shoulders loose, water bottle dripping condensation down his glove—but Mae could tell it was a façade. He was coiled tight as a starter spring. Mae stood a few feet away, VIP lanyard swinging against her ribs, pretending to scroll her phone. She'd braced for heightened attention this weekend, but nothing prepared her for the hum of being *noticed*—catalogued, whispered about. Still, she kept her chin lifted. Until **he** arrived.

Ryder Knox entered like a storm cell: the air changed, people instinctively stepped aside. He wasn't taller than Trace, but everything about him felt overbuilt—black gear pants hanging low on lean hips, sleeveless team tank showing tattooed biceps coiled with snakes and piston art, a smirk carved for tabloids. Mae's pulse thrummed. "*That's him, isn't it?*" she murmured. Trace didn't break posture. "Yep. Ryder **fucking** Knox." The swear landed like gravel between his teeth. Ryder's gaze slid over Trace—dismissive—then latched onto Mae. He zeroed in with a slow, predatory grin.

"**Well, well,**" he drawled, voice rich as bourbon. "Trace Jagger. Didn't expect to see you smiling this much during press week." Trace's reply was deadpan ice. "Didn't expect to see you still riding after all that smoke you ate last season." A few reporters nearby sucked in a breath. Ryder chuckled, low and dangerous. "Cute. *Real* cute." His eyes tracked Mae, deliberate and unhurried—taking in the loose waves of her hair, the curve of her mouth, the lanyard that marked her as Trace's guest. Heat crawled up her neck, part adrenaline, part irritation. "And you must be the reason he's riding like he's got something to lose," Ryder said, head cocked. "Whole damn paddock's talking about the new good-luck charm." Mae folded her arms. "Depends. Are you always this forward with strangers, or is today special?" "Just observant," Ryder answered, gaze unflinching. "You glow like a good fuck *and* a bad idea." Trace moved—one step forward, jaw flexing. "Easy, Knox." Ryder didn't blink. If anything, his smile spread wider, shark-bright. He leaned closer, voice dropping so only they could hear. "Six months, Jagger. We're sharing every gate drop. Let's hope your pretty distraction doesn't cost you the title—" his eyes flicked briefly to Mae's lips "—or cost *her* something worse." The implied threat was velvet-soft, razor-sharp.

Trace's shoulders went stone. Mae felt the ripple of rage roll off him. Without thinking, she slipped her hand into his—not because she was afraid, but because he looked a half-second from swinging. Ryder's gaze dipped to their linked fingers; he winked, slow and mocking, then turned on his heel and strolled away like a man who'd lit a fuse just to watch it burn. Silence swelled between them, thick with unsaid things. Trace exhaled, the breath whistling through his teeth. "He's not gonna get in my head," he muttered, squeezing her hand hard enough she felt his pulse. Mae squeezed back. "He tried and failed. Let's keep it that way."

But Trace didn't relax. If anything, his jaw set harder. They made it back to his trailer, and the silence lingered even after the door closed behind them. He peeled off his gloves, one finger at a time, and dropped them onto the table. "He's just trying to get in my head. He always does this before the circuit begins." "Did it ever work before?" Mae asked, crossing her arms. Trace looked at her. "It never mattered before." That hit her square in the chest. She walked to him, wrapping her arms around his waist. "You've got me, Jagger. But I'm not a liability. Don't treat me like one." His arms came around her fast, strong, grounding. "I know. I don't. I just... he'll dig. He always does. He doesn't care who he hurts to get under my skin." Mae pulled back just enough to meet his eyes. "Then don't let him." They stood there a while—touch anchoring them while the world outside ticked forward.

Later, Trace had to head out for an equipment check. Mae watched from the edge of the pit as he disappeared into the maze of trailers and track bikes. Ryder passed again. This time alone. He stopped five feet away, pretending to check a message on his phone. "You're not scared of me," he said quietly, still not looking at her. "No," Mae replied. "But you *should* be scared of how much I'm willing to protect him." That earned a glance. Sharp. Intrigued. "Well damn. Jagger picked a firecracker." Mae stepped forward. "Keep testing him, Knox. But don't come near me again. One threat was enough." He gave a lazy, slow smile. "Not a threat, sweetheart. Just a forecast. Storm's coming. You can feel it, right?" Mae didn't answer. She turned and walked away. But the words stayed. Storm's coming. And she felt it, too.

By the time the interviews wrapped, Trace was quieter. Less joking. Hyper-focused. Mae recognized that armor; she'd worn versions of it herself. They walked toward the trailer, dusk painting the sky a bruised orange. Trace kept her hand in his stride, purposeful, jaw set. Mae glanced sidelong. "Talk to me." Trace shook his head once. "Later. After I smoke him tomorrow." And Mae realized: this wasn't just about racing anymore. This was war.

Chapter 31

Heat Check

The day of the qualifying heat arrived under a blistering sky. The sun beat down on the paddock, baking the asphalt and igniting the air with the scent of fuel, sweat, and adrenaline. Mae stood on the sidelines, her lanyard damp with humidity and nerves, watching as Trace mounted his bike with surgical focus. Trace looked every bit the part: gear snug, helmet clipped, jaw set like concrete. The chatter around them faded when he fired up the engine. Mae felt her chest vibrate with it, a deep, guttural growl that mirrored the tension in her spine. Tori had texted that morning:

Tori: Remember, deep breaths. And don't punch anyone unless they punch first.

Mae had laughed, but her fingers were still clenched around the rail now, nails pressing into her palm. This wasn't just a race. This was *the* race—the first head-to-head between Trace and Ryder since their near collision last season. The gates dropped. Trace launched. For the first lap, he rode smooth and sharp, cutting inside corners, skimming the top of jumps with signature precision. Mae barely breathed. Ryder loomed behind him like a shadow with teeth, always just close enough to threaten. Fans roared. Pit crews shouted. Midway through lap three, Ryder clipped Trace's back tire on a corner. Mae gasped. Trace wobbled but recovered in a blink. The officials didn't throw a flag. It looked like an accident. But Mae saw the smirk Ryder shot over his shoulder. "Asshole," she muttered under her breath.

Trace didn't retaliate. He pulled ahead, aggressive and fluid, reclaiming his lead by the final lap. When he crossed the finish line first, the stands erupted. Mae clapped both hands over her mouth, stunned and buzzing with relief. He'd done it. He'd held his ground.

The roar of the engine still echoed in Trace's bones. The win hadn't just been a statement—it had been a punch to the chest, a *fuck you* to every doubt Ryder Knox tried to plant. When the checkered flag dropped, Trace didn't raise his fists in the air or wheelie across the line. He simply rode straight to the pit and peeled off his helmet, eyes scanning until he found her. Mae. She stood just past the fence, pressed between security and a wave of fans, smiling like she'd swallowed sunlight. Her hair was a mess from the wind, her lips parted in disbelief. Trace vaulted the barrier before anyone could stop him and caught her around the waist. "You're insane," she breathed into his chest. He grinned, burying his face in her shoulder. "Did I scare you?" "A little. But I think I liked it." His fingers found her waist. "Don't say things like that unless you want to be late to the awards ceremony." "Tempting." He kissed her neck, slow and dirty, and for a second, the tension evaporated. The world blurred. Just him, her, and the thrum of adrenaline between them.

Back at the trailer, the celebration was a blur of back slaps, beer cans cracked open, and mechanics yelling over each other about torque ratios and traction gains. Mae lingered at the edge of the noise, watching

Trace with a quiet pride that caught in her throat. He eventually pulled her into the tiny back room—barely big enough for a cot and a gear rack—and closed the door behind them. "I needed to see you," he said, voice rough. "I'm right here."

He kissed her then, hard and desperate, like he hadn't just seen her five minutes ago. Her back hit the wall, his hands found her hips, and the heat between them reignited. "Say it again," he whispered against her mouth. "That I like it?" "Yeah. That you liked seeing me like that. Mean. Reckless. Winning for *you*." She tangled her fingers in his hair, pulling him closer. "I loved it. All of it. Even the part where I almost passed out because I forgot to breathe." He growled—a low, satisfied sound—and nipped at her collarbone. "Careful, Flip-Flops. I might get used to that look on your face." "Then earn it." He did. Right there, against the gear rack, hands under her shirt, mouths moving like they were trying to erase the world. They didn't have much time before the awards call, but Trace made every second count.

Afterward, flushed and still half-wrecked, Mae fixed her hair while Trace tugged on a fresh shirt and smirked at her in the mirror. "You coming up with me?" Mae arched her brow. "You want the crowd seeing you with your 'pretty distraction' on the podium?" He stepped behind her, wrapped his arms around her waist, and kissed her temple. "I want the whole damn world to know. Let them talk." And when Trace took the podium, the first-place trophy raised high under the arena lights, his eyes found Mae instantly. No wink this time. No joke. Just a look that said everything. This one's for you. All of it is. And the storm? Let it come. But later, when Trace was called away to debrief with his team, Mae sat alone near the trailer. Her phone buzzed.

Unknown number: You make a hell of a trophy.

Her stomach flipped. She stared at the message, pulse thudding. Another ping.

Unknown number: He can win today. But six months is a long time.

Mae's throat tightened. She looked up across the paddock. Ryder Knox was watching her. And smiling.

Chapter 32

Tether

The sponsor dinner that night was held in a sleek, candlelit courtyard beneath hanging bulbs and high expectations. The tables were dressed in crisp linens, centerpieces made of dark greenery and gold-dipped roses. Waitstaff moved like clockwork, offering glasses of champagne and artfully plated hors d'oeuvres. Trace cleaned up into a dark button-down and jeans, the kind that looked effortless but probably cost too much. Mae wore black—simple, stunning—and smiled through introductions and camera flashes. Her heels clicked like punctuation against the stone floor as she followed Trace through circles of suits and sports media.

The food was good, the champagne better, and the setting surreal. Trace looked like he belonged here—comfortable under spotlight, charismatic with executives, magnetic in every room. Mae couldn't stop glancing at him. Every now and then, he'd catch her eye and wink, like she was the only real thing in the crowd. But the conversation at the head table shifted when a rep from the European division stood up and raised his glass. "To bold moves and international legends in the making. We'd love to officially welcome Trace Jagger to the Euro Circuit. Six months.

Full sponsorship. Bigger venues. Bigger prizes." A ripple of polite applause followed. Forks paused mid-air. Glasses clinked. And Mae felt it—the shift in the air, like a punch to the gut masked by polished smiles. Six months. Overseas. Same circuit as Ryder Knox.

Trace leaned toward her, voice low. "I didn't know they'd announce it tonight." Mae kept her face neutral, her posture perfect. "Congratulations." "Mae—" "I'm proud of you. Really." And she meant it. But beneath the proud, beneath the poised, something cracked. Just a little. Not enough to show. Just enough to feel. The rest of the dinner passed in a blur—more smiles, more clinks of glass, and Mae fighting the ache in her chest. She caught Ryder across the courtyard once, smirking at her like he already knew. Like he'd been waiting for this moment.

Later, in the quiet of the parking lot, Mae stood beside the truck while Trace shook hands and accepted final goodbyes. His silhouette was sharp against the glow of outdoor sconces, suit jacket slung over his shoulder, confidence wrapped around him like smoke. When he joined her, she smiled again—soft and private. "You should do it," she said before he could speak. "Are you sure?" "No." She laughed, but it wasn't sharp. It was honest. "But it's not really a question, is it? You were made for this." He reached for her hand. "So were you. For this life. This chaos." She met his eyes, and for a moment, she let him see the crack. The fear that came with wanting someone this much. The ache that bloomed when you realized you couldn't hold the clock still. "Just promise you won't forget who's waiting at the end of it."

Trace kissed her then—not for show, not for noise. Just for her. Just to say he wouldn't. His lips were soft but certain. His hand against her jaw steady. And for one breath, one quiet, golden second—Mae believed it. But she couldn't stop the quiet ache in her chest. The distance was coming. The clock had started. And no one ever said how long you could hold on before something slips through your fingers.

Chapter 33

The Long Goodbye

Dinner was chaos in the best way—boxes of pizza, juice boxes, and Trace helping Beckett build a napkin fort in the middle of Mae's living room. It wasn't fancy. It wasn't planned. But it felt like something solid, something worth remembering. Mae sat cross-legged on the floor, laughing as Beckett demanded Trace try a bite of his very specific pepperoni-only slice. Trace took a dramatic bite, exaggerated a satisfied groan, and gave Beckett a fist bump that made the kid beam.

Later, after dessert and a superhero movie that none of them actually finished, Beckett crawled into Trace's lap with sleepy eyes and a yawn the size of Texas. "You have to win," he mumbled, pressing his cheek to Trace's shoulder. Trace smiled, smoothing a hand down Beckett's back. "That's the plan, buddy. You're gonna cheer for me from here?" Beckett nodded, then slipped something off his wrist. A braided band of red and black string, frayed at the edges but clearly well-loved. "For luck," he said, handing it over. Trace looked at it like Beckett had handed him the keys to the kingdom. He tied it around his own wrist without hesitation. "Then I can't lose." Mae didn't say anything. She couldn't. The lump in her throat was too big.

After Beckett was tucked in with extra kisses and whispered jokes, Mae found Trace on the back porch. The stars were bright, lazy above them, the kind of night sky that dared you to believe in something. He reached for her hand without looking. She laced their fingers together. "I wish I didn't have to go," he said quietly. "I wish I didn't want you to go so badly," she whispered. "But I do. And that's the problem." He kissed the back of her hand. "I'll come back. You know that, right?" She nodded, even if she didn't feel it all the way down. "I want to believe it."

They didn't talk much. Just held onto each other like time would stop if they gripped hard enough. When they finally made it to bed, it wasn't about sex or words. It was about memory. The feel of his mouth, the weight of his body, the way his hand pressed to her back like he could anchor her there forever. He didn't rush. He didn't joke. He made love to her like it was the last night of something sacred. Like the sound of her gasp and the way she whispered his name would be the only things to keep him grounded across time zones and oceans. He touched her like she was his map home.

Mae clung to him, memorizing every kiss, every breath, every hushed word that hovered between them. Her nails dragged along his shoulder blades. His hands splayed over her ribs. They moved like they didn't want it to end—like they could stretch the night into something eternal. He whispered to her—not sweet nothings, but truths. That he didn't want to leave. That he'd count the hours. That no one else had ever made him feel like this. And when it was over, they stayed wrapped around each other. No shift in weight. No letting go. They didn't sleep much. When they did, it was tangled and restless. Her face was buried in his neck. His fingers curled protectively at her hip. A kind of sleep that wasn't really sleep—just a fragile surrender.

The airport came too fast. Trace looked stupidly good in his hoodie and ballcap, duffel slung over his shoulder. Mae wore sunglasses she didn't need indoors, and Beckett carried a dinosaur backpack and a juice pouch he refused to finish. The gate announcement echoed through the terminal. "Final boarding for Flight 176 to Zurich." Trace knelt in front of Beckett. "You holding it down while I'm gone?" Beckett nodded solemnly. "We'll still watch your races. And I'll boo that guy you don't like." Trace laughed, hugged him tight. "Good man." Then it was just Mae. She stepped into his arms, the chaos of the terminal fading around them. He held her like a lifeline. Like he needed her breath to breathe. "I hate this," she whispered. "I know."

He kissed her hard. Not just a goodbye. A promise. A prayer. Something wordless and infinite. His mouth moved over hers like he was memorizing it—like each brush of lips, each press of tongue, was a tether he couldn't afford to lose. Her hands fisted in the back of his shirt, knuckles white. She tasted salt—hers or his, she didn't know—and he kissed her like a man on borrowed time. When they finally broke apart, it wasn't distance that settled between them. It was devotion. He pressed their foreheads together, breath shaking. "Say it. One more time." Mae swallowed hard, her voice the softest weapon. "Don't forget to come back to me." Trace nodded once, tightly. "Never." Then he was gone. She stood at the window with Beckett beside her, watching the plane taxi onto the runway, sunglasses hiding her eyes, heart raw. As the engines roared and the plane lifted into the sky, Mae whispered again—quieter this time, like it hurt to say: "Don't forget to come back to me." And the sky didn't answer. But she hoped he heard it anyway.

Chapter 34

Signal Lost

Week One was fire. Their phones barely left their hands. Time zones were irrelevant when desire was that loud. They FaceTimed from hotel rooms, backstage corners, and after dark in Mae's bed with the sheets tangled around her thighs. Laughter poured like wine. Dirty talk burned through the battery. They were on each other like a second skin—even if it was only glass and signal. One night, after Mae had slipped into one of Trace's hoodies and nothing else, she sent a photo. Just a flash of her thigh.

Mae:
You're just horny.

Trace:
Yeah.
For you.
Only you.

Mae:
Sure it's not jet lag?

Sleep deprivation?
The thousands of fans screaming your name?

Trace:
None of them sound like you when you come.
None of them say my name like it's a goddamn religion.
You ruined me.

Mae:
You remember last night?
Porch. My bed. That thing you whispered against my thigh?

Trace:
Every second.
The taste of you.
The way your breath hitched when I told you to hold still.
How your fingers tangled in the sheets like you were trying to survive me.

Mae:
I was.
I didn't want to forget.

Trace:
I didn't want to leave.
But now all I think about is fucking you slow enough to memorize your soul.

Mae:
I'm not wearing anything under this shirt.
I wore it to bed because it smells like you.
I can't stop touching myself when I wear it.

Trace:
Fuck.
Tell me how.
Right now.

Mae:
One hand. Between my thighs.
The other one, holding this damn phone.
You want details?

Trace:
Yes.
Every single one.
I want to hear the way you moan when you slide that hand lower.
I want to hear how wet you are.
I want you to whisper my name like I'm still in the room.
Like I never left.

Mae:
It's already there.
Soaked.
And I haven't even touched my clit yet.
Still think this is jet lag?

Trace:
You know what I'd do if I was there?

Mae:
Yes.
But tell me anyway.

Trace:
I'd pin your wrists above your head and make you beg.
I'd keep you on the edge for hours.
I'd fuck you slow until your voice broke on my name.
Then fast. Until your legs gave out.
Until the neighbors knew who you belonged to.

Mae:
I'm already there.
Say it again.

Trace:
You're mine.
You've always been mine.
Say it back.

Mae:
I'm yours.
Only yours.

The screen dimmed. The call icon lit up. Her heart stuttered as she answered, barely whispering his name. And for a little while, the miles disappeared. She came undone with his voice in her ear, his name in her mouth, and the ache of missing him buried deep in her chest. They didn't say goodbye after. Just heavy breathing. Quiet. Until he finally murmured, "I need you, Mae. In every fucking way." She didn't respond. But in the silence, he knew she felt it too.

Week Two, they still burned. The distance hurt, but the want was louder. They called nightly, voices low in the dark. Some nights were soft, sweet confessions and laughter. Others were laced with tension, rough with need. Mae whispered his name while he talked her through it—exactly how to touch herself, where to press, when to slow. He groaned when she moaned, cursed when she came undone with his voice in her ear. He told her what he'd do when he got back. She promised to make it worth the wait. It became a ritual. Midnight confessions. Bodies alone. Souls still entangled. He told her he wanted to map every inch of her again. Said he dreamed about her thighs, her mouth, the exact way her back arched when he hit the right spot. She told him she'd bought a new set of lingerie and refused to wear it until he was the one to take it off. Their calls ended with panting silence, raw honesty, and promises neither of them dared put into full words. But the intent hung thick between them: Don't let this be the thing that breaks us.

Week Three, the headlines exploded.

MOTO MAG: **RIVALRY REIGNITES — KNOX BUMPS JAGGER IN PRACTICE, FANS RIOT ONLINE**

SportsNow: **Slow-Mo Clip Shows Jagger's Rear Wheel Lift After Contact — Is Knox Pushing Limits or Crossing Lines?**

Sports blogs. Paparazzi snapshots of scratched plastics and angry hand gestures. Talk-show segments dissecting Trace's body language frame by frame. Mae watched one clip on mute and felt her stomach flip at the grind of metal against dirt. Trace's replies came slower. Briefer. More distracted.

Mae:
Saw the footage. Are you hurt?

Trace (audio voicemail, raspy):
Bruised hip. Grip burn on my palm. Nothing broken.

Trying to learn the new track lines.
Call you after an ice bath. Promise.

    Five hours. No call. A blurry selfie finally arrived: Trace shirtless, purple bruise blooming at his ribs, thumbs-up that looked forced.

Mae:
Wish I could kiss it better.

Trace:
Soon.
Film review now. Need to find an extra tenth in the whoops.
Miss your voice.

She sent a thirty-second voice note: soft, encouraging, ending with *"Win for you, come home for me."* He heart-reacted. That night she waited with the phone on her pillow. Midnight passed. 1 a.m. passed. At 2:17 a.m. a single notification lit the screen: 🖤 No call. No goodnight. The phone felt heavier than ever.

Week Four, she was talking to a ghost.

Mae:
Miss you.

Eighteen hours later: 🖤

She scrolled back through older messages just to hear his voice in her head. Just to remember what it felt like to be needed.

    Week Five, there was nothing. No pings. No calls. No replies. Just silence. Mae lay on the couch alone, scrolling their old texts, thumb hovering over the screen. She paused on a photo of his hand on her thigh. Another of him, sleeping in her bed, bare chest rising and falling. She didn't cry. Not yet. But the ache was there. Loud. Empty. And growing.

Chapter 35

Final Lap

Mae stood in the small break-room kitchen at work, staring into a mug of lukewarm coffee she hadn't taken a sip of. The smell turned her stomach. Again. Fatigue clung to her like a second skin—heavy and inescapable. Every night ended with her scrolling through old messages while the house settled into quiet. Every morning began with nausea she blamed on stress and bad sleep. Tori noticed first. They were unpacking new inventory at the boutique when Mae rubbed a hand across her belly and winced. "Uh, hon," Tori said, ducking around a stack of shoeboxes. "Not to pry, but... when was your last period?" Mae opened her mouth. Closed it. Blinked. Calendar math flickered behind her eyes and landed on a date that felt far away. "Oh," she managed. "Yeah," Tori said gently. "Oh."

The boutique was slow that day—soft gray light leaking through the windows, the air thick with late-afternoon lull and the faint scent of lavender cleaner. Customers moved like background actors: polite smiles, occasional questions, no urgency. It should've been peaceful. But Mae felt like she was underwater. She moved on autopilot, fingers folding scarves that didn't need folding, retagging the same rack twice. She restocked a display of perfume bottles, each clink of glass against wood sounding too sharp. Tori asked a question about inventory, and Mae nodded like she'd heard. But she hadn't. Her body was in the shop. Her mind was somewhere else entirely—lost in the echo chamber of a future she hadn't asked for, one she wasn't ready to name out loud. **What does this mean for Beckett?** That was the first loop. The one that came with guilt curled tight like a fist in her stomach. He'd just gotten used to Trace. To routine. To quiet mornings and steady hands pouring cereal and tucking him into bed. She'd promised stability. Promised she wouldn't let anyone shake his world again. And now, her body was rewriting all of it.

What happens if Trace finds out and doesn't want this? That was the second loop. More jagged. Trace had been distant lately—radio silent for over a week. Maybe it was the stress. The rivalry. The media whirlwind. But maybe it was something else. Maybe he felt the pull of another life. A life without her. A life where a baby didn't fit. **What if he does want it... and it still doesn't work?** She didn't know which was worse—that he might not want this, or that he would. That he'd fly across an ocean, say the right things, try to make it work... only for everything to fall apart under the weight of trying too hard. **What if she tells him and it becomes a burden?** Would he feel trapped? Obligated? Would the freedom he fought so hard to ride toward suddenly feel like a cage? Would he come back... and then resent her for the reason?

What if she doesn't... and that becomes the regret? Would she look into the baby's eyes years from now and wonder? Would she let Trace's memory be a shadow instead of a presence? Would she be rewriting the same mistakes she swore she'd never repeat? The questions didn't come one at a time. They overlapped. Collided. Spun together like a storm. She tried to ground herself with tasks—straightening hangers, refolding sweaters, pretending she didn't feel like the floor might open up beneath her. Tori said something about closing early, about the clouds rolling in. Mae nodded. But her hands were trembling.

She slipped into the stockroom, just for a moment. Leaned against the wall beside the breaker box and slid her palms over the slight curve of her stomach. It wasn't visible. Not yet. But she felt it anyway. It wasn't a bump. It was a presence. A tether to something that hadn't even formed fingers yet—and still, it felt like everything. She closed her eyes and tried to breathe. **This chaos had a heartbeat.** Not just her own. A second one. A softer thrum tucked inside her. She didn't know if it was a boy or girl. Didn't know the due date or how she'd manage doctor's appointments with her shifts. Didn't know if she'd cry the first time she heard it kick. But she knew this much: she wasn't alone anymore. And that changed everything.

She bought the test on her lunch break. One of those digital ones, because she couldn't stand the ambiguity of faint lines or cheap dye. Her hands trembled the entire walk home. She didn't rush. She didn't wait either. The bathroom was quiet when she closed the door behind her. She set the box down, peeled off the foil, read the instructions twice even though she already knew. Then she peed. Then she waited. Her thoughts spun like a carousel of memories. Trace's grin. Beckett's laugh. That last night. The porch. The whisper. The ache. When the timer buzzed, she didn't move right away. But then she did. Mae stepped forward and looked down. She set the stick on the counter, watched the second line bloom, and felt the future tilt on its axis.

That night, she didn't call anyone. Didn't tell Tori. Didn't cry. She made tea. Put Beckett to bed. Curled on the couch with the throw blanket and flipped on the TV. A motocross stream was live—Euro Circuit, round five. Bright lights, roaring crowds, commentary breaking down stats in clipped, excited tones. They panned to the lineup. Trace. Number 42. Helmet low. Shoulders squared. Mae pressed a hand to her stomach. The touch was soft. Protective. She didn't move. Didn't blink. But her free hand reached for the phone on the coffee table. She opened their chat—her last message *Miss you* still hanging lonely above the red heart he'd sent weeks ago. Her thumbs hovered. *I'm pregnant.* She stared at the three words until they blurred. Deleted them. Tried again. *We need to talk.* Deleted. *Be safe tonight.* She almost sent that—simple, harmless—but the harmlessness stung. She backed out of the keyboard and locked the screen. On-camera, Trace and Ryder rolled their bikes onto the grid. An interviewer jogged up with a mic. Trace flipped his visor up to answer. Instinct screamed. Mae unlocked her phone, typed fast:

Mae:
Trace... I have news. Big news. Call me after the race. Please.

She hit send before she could change her mind. The camera caught Trace's phone pressed into his pit tech's hand. He glanced down at the screen—her message lighting up in bold white—then back at the interviewer. A flicker crossed his face. Jaw tense. Eyes narrowing—confusion? Fear? She couldn't tell. He tucked the phone under a towel on the handlebars, gave a tight nod to the mic, and the countdown clock started.

Mae's pulse hammered as the gate dropped. Laps blurred. Dirt flew. She watched him carve corners with surgical precision—and yet every time the drone camera swooped in, she searched his visor for... something. A crack. A tell. He won by half a second. Raised the trophy without a smile. The broadcast cut to post-race interviews. Trace wiped sweat from his brow, accepted the mic. The reporter asked about Knox, about strategy. Trace's gaze flicked toward the paddock entrance—where his phone no doubt waited. "Just wanted a clean race," he said, voice rough. "Got things on my mind back home." Mae's breath caught. Back on her couch, hand on her stomach, she whispered into the quiet living room: "Come back to us." She wasn't sure if she meant herself and Beckett, or the new life fluttering just beneath her skin. Maybe all of them. Either way, the message was out there now—waiting, like she was—for whatever came next.

Made in United States
Orlando, FL
13 July 2025